The Prada Plan 4:

Love & War

The Prada Plan 4:

Love & War

Ashley Antoinette

www.urbanbooks.net

Urban Books, LLC
97 N18th Street
Wyandanch, NY 11798

The Prada Plan 4: Love & War Copyright © 2014
Ashley Antoinette

ISBN 13: 978-1-60162-580-9
ISBN 10: 1-60162-580-4

First Trade Paperback Printing July 2014
Printed in the United States of America

10 9 8 7 6

Distributed by Kensington Publishing Corp.
Submit Wholesale Orders to:
Kensington Publishing Corp.
C/O Penguin Group (USA) Inc.
Attention: Order Processing
405 Murray Hill Parkway
East Rutherford, NJ 07073-2316
Phone: 1-800-526-0275
Fax: 1-800-227-9604

The Prada Plan 4:

Love & War

From the beautiful mind of . . . *Ashley Antoinette*

"I dedicate this book to love because I know that it has the power to triumph over all things that stand in its way . . ."

—Ashley Antoinette Coleman

Acknowledgments

Always first and foremost, I have to thank God for the consistency of His grace, of His mercy, and of His blessings. I would be nothing without Him and I am eternally grateful for the beautiful way in which he designed my destiny. I am humbled by the fact that I always come out victorious, but I know that it is only because of His guidance and unconditional love for me.

To my husband. I love you. I love you forever and a day. I am so proud of our bond. It has proved strong and unbreakable. The fact that our souls are so perfectly aligned gives me chills. You are the wind beneath my wings and you encourage me to soar to new heights, while keeping your arms wide open just in case I fall. I am fearless because I know I have your protection. My heart beats for you. I am your 'Diz'. You are my 'babe'. Our friendship is the greatest foundation for our infinite love. I don't think that it is possible to have a deeper connection than the one we share. We are twelve years into this thing with forever to go and I'm so excited to grow old with you. We have been through it all and we're still here. That's the thing about destiny . . . nothing can alter this path we're walking together. God built us as a pair. I love you. I am you. You are me. We are forever one. My nigga. Last name Coleman.

To my son, MY EVERYTHING. You bring me so much joy. It is because of you and you alone that I am so strong. Your spirit has been the fuel that keeps me going. You are so pure, so untainted by the world. Seeing you experience life is such a blessing. Its like you give me a chance to see things for the first time again. Everything is more beautiful because of you. You make me slow down and appreciate each moment. Life is so exciting for you and I am so blessed to be able to guide you as you grow and learn. You are my heart. There is no measuring my love for you. It just is and it will forever be. The best parts of your father and I is in your DNA. I see greatness in you and I can't wait until you make your mark on the world. You are a future king. I am so grateful for you, Quaye "Tip" Coleman. My miracle.

To my mommy, the older I get the more I appreciate everything that you have done for me. I love you. Our bond is sacred and unconditional. I know if nobody has my back, you do . . . right or wrong. There is nothing like a mother's love and if I don't tell you enough, you are amazing.

To my fans! I could just scream!!!! Fans? I have them? Like, seriously! You all have been on this ride with me for so long. You are my day 1's! My supporters! My motivators! Hell, even my critics sometimes! Each and every one of you make me a better writer. I appreciate you for the e-mails, the Twitter and Facebook messages, the encouraging words and your undying support. You guys go hard for me and I have to acknowledge you. Without you there would be no me. I do this for you and I thank you from the bottom of my heart.

To the girls I can't possibly live without. Sydney, Ashley M., Shonda, and Char. I love you. You all are my sisters whether by blood or by love. I simply cannot ever see life without you all in it. You each fill my life with love, support, and laughter. We will share a bond forever. Thank you for being my true blues.

Chapter 1

Indie stood outside of the church feeling defeated as he realized that YaYa had stood him up. At this moment they were supposed to be newlyweds and indulging in happiness as they embarked on a new life together, but instead they were as distant as strangers. Lately they had been like oil and water. No matter how much they tried to see eye to eye, they didn't mix. Her issue with drugs, her history with Leah, and her new addiction to money and power were all wearing on Indie. He loved YaYa with every inch of him. She was his rib. Her smile warmed him like rays from the sun. He loved the shit out of her in all honesty, but it was always so hard for her to give him her all. Did he feel her love? Yes, he believed that she loved him in her own way, but she came with so much baggage and too many skeletons. He had been willing to put up with a lot but he was beginning to grow impatient. He couldn't wait for this one woman forever. Either they got it right or it was time for them to say their good-byes and search for normalcy apart. Indie's heart ached as the thought of moving on from the love of his life entered his mind. He wanted to be with this one woman forever but she was elusive, her ability to hold him down uncertain and their future dismal.

Chase emerged from the small white chapel and descended the steps. The tailored suit he wore bossed up his appearance as he approached Indie, his hands tucked in his pockets. Sympathy was written all over his face.

"I've tried calling her, bro, it's going straight to voice-mail," Chase stated.

"We fought last night," Indie explained. His voice was calm and indifferent, but his pain was evident. He was a man burdened by love. That one emotion had brought many men to their knees and Indie was beginning to feel the burden of it as his resilience to disappointment began to dwindle. His shoulders slumped as if he carried the weight of the world on top of them and the burning sting of loss shone in his eyes. The lump in his throat changed the inflection in his tone. Anyone who knew him well could see and hear that he was hurt. "I called the wedding off after I found out you were telling the truth about her and the drugs. I ran out on her."

Chase pulled out a Benz key from his pocket and deactivated the alarm on his S-Class. "Hop in, I'll take you back to grab your phone from Mom dukes. After that we'll head over to the house to see if she's there," Chase said, taking the lead because he could tell that his big homie wasn't in the right state of mind to do it himself.

"I'm taking orders from you now?" Indie said with a smirk, but with pride in his voice. He had groomed Chase. Everything that Chase was, Indie had made him. He had schooled him on the game, on manhood, on life and Chase had been a quick study. He was a boss in his own right. The young boy he witnessed being chased off the block in Houston was now a grown man who was fully capable of running an empire.

"Hop in, big homie," Chase said with a half smile as he shook his head shyly.

Indie turned to his mother who was emerging from the small chapel with the rest of the guests. She held his daughter in her arms while looking at him with worried eyes. "What are you going to do?" Elaine asked. Concern shone in her eyes and her brows dipped low as she stared at her only living son. Indie could see her worry but he couldn't make her any guarantees. He lived for YaYa and would undoubtedly die for her as well. Their love was a tragic one, never perfect, but unending. It was their imperfections that made them who they were, but they were symbiotic. One needed the other to survive. Her destruction would ultimately lead to his own and if she walked out his life today it would ruin him forever. There wasn't a doubt in his mind that his woman would be his demise. He would either kill over her, for her, or die because of her. Either way it was all worth the short time that he got to experience her love. She was nothing short of amazing and he just wanted to let her know. Now was not the time to walk away. They weren't at the end game. True, times had been rough, but their love story was just beginning. Indie kissed his mother on the forehead gently and vaguely replied, "Whatever I have to do." He couldn't give her a definitive answer because he had no idea where YaYa was. Was she in trouble? Was she scared? Did she runaway from him? Was she angry? High? Indie didn't know but he knew that anything was possible when it came to her. He placed his car key into Elaine's palm and kissed Skylar's cheek. "Take care of her for me. I'll swing by to get her as soon as I find out what's going on."

Indie slid into Chase's luxury whip and glanced at his daughter through the side mirror as they drove away. He came up off his hip with the burner and without even asking Chase punched in a code on his dash to pop out the hidden console. Indie placed the weapon inside as he melted into the butter leather seat. He rubbed his temple as stress pulsed through his body. Indie appreciated the silence as Chase chauffeured him through the streets. They had been rocking long enough for Chase to know when his input was needed and now was not the time. Indie's mental was drained. Trying to maintain sanity with a love affair as insane as the one he and Disaya shared was impossible. Whenever anything similar to normalcy appeared in their lives, chaos soon interrupted. Cotton ball-sized snowflakes fell outside of his window, blanketing the world in soft whiteness, making it seem less cruel. The winter wonderland would have been the perfect backdrop for them to confirm their union before God. Instead, it felt like a cold joke as YaYa's absence froze his bleeding heart. He was ready to pull back. Shorty had him open and too emotional for his liking. Indie had always been levelheaded and calculating, but he couldn't focus when his emotions were off kilter. When YaYa plagued his heart he felt lovesick and nothing but her affection could heal that.

Chase pulled up to Elaine's home and Indie braved the winter storm as he hopped out. The snow was so deep that the Prada dress shoes he wore sank into it as he made his way to the door. He entered, retrieved his phone in haste then bolted back out to the car.

"Did she call?" Chase asked before pulling away.

Indie powered on his phone and it illuminated instantly with a voice message. The words My World was accompanied by a picture of YaYa and Skylar on the screen. He had saved her number under the endearing term so that each time she called he was reminded of what he had to lose if he ever slipped up in the streets. He checked the time, noticing that she had called the night before. In the heat of their fight he had turned off his phone. He hadn't wanted to be reached but now he wished that he had kept the line of communication open. He placed the phone to his ear as he played back her message: "You bitch. We get burnt by the same fucking fire and you come out just fine, while I'm left looking like this!"

Indie frowned when he heard Leah's voice screaming in anger on his voicemail and his heart dropped instantly as he pressed the phone against his ear.

"You ruined my life." It was YaYa's voice he heard in response now. "If I die tonight, you're dying with me. You pull that trigger and I lose control of the car. You came here to kill me, but are you ready to die?"

Indie gripped his phone as he hit the dashboard in frustration while terror seized his heart. The realization of what had happened hit him like a ton of bricks. YaYa hadn't left him at the altar because she didn't want to be there. She couldn't be there. She had been trapped in Leah's clutches and this time he wasn't so sure that she had survived.

Chapter 2

Indie always knew what to do. He always planned the moves he made to ensure that he made no mistakes, but in this moment he was lost. He didn't know what move came next. Panic seared through him as a fear like none he had ever felt before invaded his psyche.

"Leah's got her," Indie said in a low tone as regret seized the moment and his chest clenched painfully. It felt like he was choking as he grabbed at the bowtie around his neck. He squeezed his phone in his hand tightly. "She called me for help last night and I shut her out," he said. His mind spun as he replayed the message in his head. It had cut off suddenly. He didn't know if YaYa was dead or alive, but his gut told him that he should fear the worst. Excruciation filled him as he tried to focus his thoughts. He immediately dialed Agent Norris. Who he had once viewed as a scumbag Fed was now his only hope in finding Disaya. Indie's problem was too difficult for him to solve alone. He didn't know where to even begin looking. Hours had passed since receiving that call. The unknown haunted him, adding to his misery as his stomach knotted from worry. As soon as Norris came on the line Indie's voice began barking off instructions.

"I need you to track a phone number for me. YaYa is missing and I think Leah is responsible," Indie said.

Norris's response came out as a whisper. "I can't just track the phone. It isn't that easy. I need approval for that type of thing," he replied, cautiously.

"Fuck your approvals, Norris. I'm not asking. She's in trouble. I need to know where she is now," Indie replied with authority. There was something about Indie that made grown men comply with little resistance. His mentality and reputation that he had acquired over the years allowed him to demand authority.

"YaYa is supposed to be dead already. You wanted it that way. I can't put a trace on woman who no longer exists," Norris whispered harshly, clearly stressed by the web that he was stuck in. He had gotten in bed with a gangster and Indie was calling in a favor.

"It may take me some time," Norris replied.

"There is no time!" Indie barked.

"Okay, okay," Norris replied. Indie could practically see him pacing back and forth. He didn't care if this was the thing that would end Norris's notable career. If Norris didn't comply Indie would end Norris's life. "I'll call you back in five minutes."

Indie couldn't get the protest out of his mouth before he heard the ring tone in his ear. "Fucking pig!" he demeaned as he hit the dashboard in frustration.

"We'll find her, bro," Chase said, speaking up for the first time. Indie appreciated Chase's silence. He had taught him that if he couldn't contribute to the solving a problem that silence and observance were the best things to provide. Although Chase had no answers, Indie knew that once he came up with one, Chase would be ready to put in work. Until then they both sat in deep contemplation, as Chase drove aimlessly through the city streets. Waiting for Norris was torture. The minutes that past felt like hours until finally Indie got the call, informing him of the location of the phone. His heart raced as he put the coordinates into his GPS and Chase drove to the destination in haste. Indie had never been overly religious but in that moment the terror that pulsed through him was enough to humble him into prayer. He had no one else to turn to. YaYa had already survived so much and he knew that no one was given this many chances to survive. She was terrified of Leah and if they had squared off again, he wasn't sure that YaYa would be the one to come out victorious.

The flashing red and blue lights broke through the darkness of the coal black sky. They could be seen from a mile away. Time froze as soon as Chase neared the scene. There were federal agents and police officers everywhere. Indie jumped out of the car before the wheels could stop spinning and he raced to the broken barrier on the side of the bridge. "YaYa!" he screamed. His voice broke through the air, frantic, gut-wrenching. The desperation echoed through the sky and he was quickly held back by officers on the scene. He pushed through the men violently. "YaYa!" His eyes scanned the area. Tire marks that had imprinted in the soft snow had been covered by the night full of falling flakes. Bloodstains marred the snow, going from the most crimson shades of red only to dilute into pink as divers went in and out of the river. The sight of the covered body lying on the stretcher caused his stomach to hollow instantly. Norris broke through the sea of Fed jackets, walking over to him in a hurry. The solemn look he held made Indie think the worst.

"Is that her?" he asked. "Is that her?" His bark was vicious but at that moment if Norris said yes, Indie had no bite to follow it. YaYa's death would end him.

Norris shook his head. "That's neither of them. Turns out some poor schmuck has been waiting to be found under these icy waters all winter. YaYa and Leah are both at Brooklyn Presbyterian. They're both hurt, really badly. You need to get there. By the time we found them they were both near death. Looks like they had one hell of a drag-out fight. I don't know if there is a winner. Sometimes everybody loses," Norris said. "I had to pull some strings to explain YaYa's reemergence. Anyone asks . . . you say she was being held in protective custody. The death stunt was for her protection. You understand?"

Indie nodded his head. He couldn't even process what he had just heard. He had too many butterflies fluttering in his chest. "Indie!" Norris said through gritted teeth. "I need your head in the game here. This is my ass on the line."

"Understood," Indie said. He extended his hand and shook with Norris before racing to the hospital. If YaYa died because he had failed to protect her, he would never forgive himself.

YaYa opened her eyes and was instantly blinded by the fluorescent hospital lights that shined above her. Her entire body was numb and she seemed to hurt all over, but she didn't care . . . she was alive. She didn't know why she was being given yet another chance, but she closed her eyes and inhaled deeply, just to feel the air hit her lungs. Death had knocked at her door more than once but she had never feared it more than when she had found herself in front of Leah's gun. Only God himself could have caused the gun to jam. It certainly wasn't Leah's sympathy that had given her another chance at life. YaYa sat up in her bed and winced as a sharp pain shot through her. She lifted the hospital gown to see that her ribs were wrapped in layer of gauze. Suddenly the door opened and a nurse entered the room.

"Good to finally see you're awake," she greeted with a smile.

YaYa looked down at her bandaged bodice and then up at the friendly Hispanic woman inquisitively.

"You broke two ribs in the crash," she explained. "You have a concussion and you were hypothermic when they pulled you out of the water. It took two hours to thaw you completely. You were like an ice cube. Your fingers and toes got the worst of it, but considering what you've been through . . . you are very lucky. I can't say the same for the other girl who they fished out."

YaYa's eyes widened in alarm. "Is she dead?"

"No, but the gunshot wound to her chest is severe. The bullet is too close to her heart to remove it. They performed surgery to close her up, but it's very painful. Not even the pain medications can numb all of what she is feeling. The worst part is she's conscious," the nurse informed. "She's right up the hall . . . room 928."

What? YaYa thought. *How the fuck does Leah keep surviving?* She felt like she and Leah were tortured souls, connected by their obsession with one another. It seemed whenever YaYa lived, Leah did as well. She wondered if she had to die in order for Leah to finally receive her fate.

She waited until she was alone before she attempted to move. Her feet felt like cement blocks and there was no sensation in her toes as she swung her legs to the side until she was standing. Tangled in the wires of the machines she was hooked up to YaYa braced herself before pulling the IV out of her arm. She opened her mouth and screamed silently as the needle came out. She searched for a bandage to stop the small trickle of blood that flowed from her arm. She pulled out every drawer until she finally found enough materials to treat herself.

A part of her heart must have frozen as she lay on the banks of the icy river. Even after Leah's gun had jammed, even after Leah had tried her hardest to ruin her life, YaYa had grabbed her as she made her way out of the sinking car. She had barely made it to the shore before she passed out beside a bleeding Leah, face down in the snow. YaYa hadn't wanted to save Leah, but rather to have visible evidence of her death. If she had left Leah in the water there wasn't a guarantee that her body would be found, leaving YaYa to always wonder. YaYa wanted to see her in a shallow grave. She had to witness that demise first-hand. It was the only reason that she had even risked her own life to bring Leah ashore. There seemed to be no end to the madness, however. Even with the gunshot to the chest, Leah had lived and YaYa refused to take anymore. She knew that there would be no peace in her world as long as Leah was in it. One of them had to go and YaYa had been through too much for it all to be for nothing.

Her feet felt like they were being stabbed with a thousand tiny pins as she made her way out of the room. It was crazy how freezing cold eventually turned into burning torture. After being submerged in freezing water and lying out on the icy riverbank for hours, she had become hypothermic. Her toes felt like they would fall off at any second. She shouldn't even have attempted to stand so soon but she didn't care. She just wanted to see Leah. YaYa wanted to set her eyes on the bitch who had taken everything from her. She didn't know what she would do when she saw her. Wait. Scratch that. She knew exactly what she would do. She would end her on sight. The time had come to cease the cat-and-mouse game. She crept through the hall, feeling invisible as the busy nurses rushed to and fro around her. It wasn't long before the limp in her walk and the instability of her condition garnered attention from one of the scrubbed workers walking by.

"Excuse me, miss, you're in no shape to be out of your room," a male physician said. His voice halted her mid-step and she weakly leaned against the wall in defeat. He was right. She could barely make it down the hall but she was too far to turn back. Years of beef had brought her to this moment and as she looked up into the dark brown eyes of the doctor who stood before her, she felt tears overcome her.

She was still so groggy from the treatment and medications that had been inserted into her veins. Her rib cage screamed in agony with every step that she took. She reached out for him, her legs barely strong enough to keep her upright. The doctor quickly picked her up off of her feet and found the nearest wheelchair to place her in.

"You're in no condition to—"

"Please," she whispered in interruption. "I was brought here with my sister. She's right up the hall in ICU. I just want to see her. I swear after that I'll go back to my room. Please take me to see her. I'll only stay a minute. She's in 928."

The doctor checked his watch as if he were pressed for time and then motioned for one of the candy stripers who were walking by in haste. "Young lady, please take this patient to 928 to visit her sister. Give her five minutes. After that take her directly back to her own room and make sure she doesn't get out of her bed." He turned to YaYa. "I'm going to personally pop in to check on you to make sure you aren't going for any more strolls, all right?"

She nodded and gave him a grateful smile as the candy striper wheeled her up the hall and into Leah's room.

YaYa gasped when she saw the condition that Leah was in. She was hooked up to so many machines. Wires and tubes went in and out of her arms and nose. In their epic battle YaYa had been injured but she had definitely come out on top. A small victory wasn't enough for her, however. She was ready to win the war. It was the only way for her to move on with her life. *The machines, the gunshot wound . . . it'll only keep Leah down for so long. She will come for me. She always comes for me,* YaYa thought. There was something about Leah's existence that made YaYa feel cornered. Even with Leah hooked up to tubes and monitors, YaYa still feared her. It was ingrained in her, like she had been conditioned to fear Leah. Like a belt acted as reinforcement to a child, YaYa was a slave to Leah's madness. It was the kind of terror that would only go away in death. Either her own or Leah's, but it was clear that coexistence was not an option. A tear escaped her eyes and she turned to the candy striper. "Can I have a minute?" she asked.

The young girl gave her a pat on the shoulder and replied, "Sure."

When YaYa was alone with Leah she stared at her, weighing the options in her mind. She was so overwhelmed with hate, with uncertainty, with terror. Leah brought out the very worst in her. She didn't want to be stuck anymore. She felt forever frozen in a sick competition with Leah. All she wanted at that moment was to be rid of the evil that had consumed her life. Gripping the wheelchair she slowly rose as she weakly made her way to the door. She clicked the lock on the door and then turned back to make the painful trip back across the room. By the time she was standing over Leah, she was exhausted. She didn't realize it but the extent of her injuries was serious and if she were not careful she would bring herself great harm through overexertion alone. YaYa reached up and turned off the monitor; then she leaned over Leah until her mouth was directly by Leah's ear. "I hope you burn in hell, you evil bitch," she said. The sound of YaYa's voice caused Leah's eyes to flutter and when YaYa wrapped her hands around Leah's neck, her eyes flew open. She tightened her grasp, stopping her airflow, automatically causing Leah's body to tense. YaYa's squeezed so tightly that there was no room to doubt the fact that Leah was about to die. Tears flooded both of their eyes as they stared at one another. Leah's heart beat as adrenaline pulsed through her. She and Leah had once been friends, they had once lived carefree, getting money together and blowing it fast until Leah's jealousy changed the course of their relationship. Now they were common enemies and as YaYa choked the life out of Leah, her entire body trembled. Leah couldn't fight back if she wanted to. So instead of resisting she gave in to YaYa and prepared for the inevitable.

A knock at the door caused YaYa to squeeze harder. She didn't have much time to finish this.

"YaYa!"

Indie's voice rang in her ear but she didn't stop. She refused to loosen her grip. "YaYa, don't do this. This isn't the time . . . or the place," he said through the door. "You do this and there is no turning back. No getting out of it. There are too many eyes in this hospital, YaYa. I lose you for good. Sky loses you."

YaYa gritted her teeth as she applied even more pressure to Leah's neck, choking her out. The severity of Leah's wounds didn't allow her to put up a fight. YaYa had the upper hand and could easily win the war, but Indie's words had not gone unheard; they were loud and clear. He had shaken her and as images of Indie and their child flashed through her mind she began to let up. If she went through with this, if she murdered Leah with her own two hands, in the midst of the busy hospital, the repercussions would be irrevocable.

"Open the door, YaYa!" Indie shouted.

YaYa released Leah and as soon as she did Leah began to choke uncontrollably as she gasped for air. "I knew you were weak," she managed to insult as she gulped desperately for oxygen to feed her starving lungs. She laughed condescendingly as she coughed into her balled fist. Each cough sent extreme pain pulsing through her, but it was better than not feeling anything at all. It was better than the death that she had narrowly evaded.

YaYa had begun to retreat but when she heard Leah's words she stopped dead in her tracks. Her hand was on the door and she looked at Indie through the rectangular window. His eyes were pleading with her, urging her to unlock the door so that he could get inside. YaYa wanted to open it and run into his arms. She wanted to let him rescue her, like always, but this wasn't his fight. He was not the one who introduced crazy into their lives. Leah had pushed her to the edge of destruction so many times and she was ready to take control back. "I'm sorry," she mouthed silently as her brow furrowed in angst. She turned back to Leah with cold determination coursing through her veins. She stood directly over her as she heard Indie begin to knock on the door.

"Somebody come open this door! Now!" She heard another voice. She recognized it as Agent Norris.

The handle rattled. There wasn't enough time to do what she meant to, but she needed to make one thing clear.

"Every time I try to give you a pass you remind me why I can't. Rest up, Leah, and enjoy your time here because as soon as you step foot outside of this hospital, I'm on your ass. You want to see the old YaYa, you've got her," she promised. YaYa flipped the switch on the machines, turning them back on just as Indie, Agent Norris, and one of the doctors burst through the door.

The bewilderment and confusion on all of their faces was evident. "What's going on in here? Why was the door locked?" the doctor demanded as he rushed to Leah's bedside and checked her vitals as he looked from Leah to YaYa.

Leah was fading in and out as YaYa turned to the doctor and said, "I needed to prey over her."

The doctor had no idea that YaYa was truly acting as a predator, but Indie and Agent Norris knew exactly what she meant. "Please, she is in no condition for visitors and you also need your rest, Ms. Morgan."

"I'll take her back to her room," one of the nurses said.

"That won't be necessary, I'm taking her home," Indie interjected.

He picked YaYa up off of her feet and she rested her head on his chest as he carried her out of the hospital. "I wanted to kill her," she whispered.

"I know," Indie said. He kissed the top of her head and didn't look back as he walked her out of the front door. Chase waited curbside and hopped out of the car when he saw Norris coming after Indie in haste.

"Mr. Perkins!" Norris shouted as he approached. Indie placed YaYa in the back seat and then met eyes with Chase.

"Drive off. Get her lost. I'll call you when I'm on my way to get the location," Indie instructed.

"I want to stay with you," YaYa protested.

"This isn't up for debate, ma, I'll catch up soon. Don't give my nigga a hard time," Indie said seriously.

"Are you going to come back for me?" she asked, concerned about the state of her relationship.

"Always," he promised as he closed the door. He hit the top of the roof, signaling for Chase to pull off. He needed for YaYa to be tucked away somewhere safe. He wanted her untouchable until he could figure out what the next move would be.

"What the hell do you think you're doing? We both know what almost happened in that room. I need to question her," Norris stated heatedly. "She's supposed to be dead and I haven't fully explained to my superiors why she isn't. YaYa and I need to be telling the same story or I lose my fucking shield! They took her prints, drew her blood, she's going to pull up in the system—"

"You tell whatever story you need to tell to make her life normal again. We faked her death for her own protection right? Witness protection. Leah was too great of a threat." He paused for a beat as he looked around before continuing. "I'm tired of my woman being a ghost. I'm tired of her living in fear. This entire thing ends now. Leah came for her! She is always going to come for her. YaYa isn't built for any of this. The game, the pressure that comes with getting this much money, the enemies . . . she can't handle it. I need her back and I need Leah gone."

"She'll be arrested for attacking YaYa, the ADA will bring charges . . ."

Indie didn't even need to have concerns about Leah. He had tried everything except eliminating the problem himself. He wasn't leaving her prosecution up to chance. After the danger she had cursed his family with he was going to take care of her personally. His bigger concern was YaYa's return. For so long she had been underground, living under an assumed name. He needed her back and more importantly he needed to remind her of the little girl from the hood who he had fallen in love with. "It's time for YaYa to come back. I'm not talking aliases and all that . . . I want Disaya Morgan, alive and well. Free from prosecution or any possible threat. What amount of money can make that happen?" he asked. "When I make her my wife I want to be speaking to Disaya, not some alias we've made up to keep her hidden from the world," Indie said.

"We do this right, Indie, my career is on the line," Norris said in a low tone as he looked around cautiously.

"I've got two million that says fuck your career. With that kind of paper you won't need that badge," Indie said.

Visibly indecisive Norris shifted in his stance as he ruffled his hair in distress. "I can draw up paperwork . . . say I was hiding her under a protection order to keep Leah Richards from finding her."

"Whatever you have to do, make it happen," Indie said. The authority in his voice left little room for rebuttal. "I'll wait for the call."

When he was finally inside the privacy of a cab he allowed himself to process everything that had just occurred. He had walked out on the love of his life, left her vulnerable, and almost lost her because of it. The thought of what could have been burned his eyes as he squeezed the bridge of his nose. He was supposed to be her protector; there was no way that Leah should have ever gotten so close. He had tried to stay out of it, tried to dismiss Leah as just a crazy, jealous ex who needed help, but it was clear that she was a threat. She was as ruthless as they came and it was time for him to intervene. Indie had never taken a shot at anyone and missed so now that his crosshairs were set, Leah would not shimmy her way out of this one alive.

Nothing but the sound of the vintage grandfather clock sounded off inside the 8,000–square foot log cabin as YaYa and Chase sat, waiting for Indie to arrive. It was a beautiful place, built from the ground up with modern finishes. It was supposed to have been the honeymoon spot for Indie and YaYa. Tucked away in the upstate mountains of New York and surrounded by nothing but vistas of snowcapped hills, it was perfect . . . or at least it would have been. Instead of making love by the crackling fireplace and celebrating their nuptials, YaYa was recovering from her run-in with her worst enemy.

"You may as well go to sleep. Get some rest. It looks like you could use it. It took us six hours to get up here. With the roads as bad as they are Indie probably won't make it until morning anyway," Chase said. He was short with her and for good reason. YaYa had snaked Chase and ruined his friendship with Indie over pure lies. She knew that he had plenty of reason not to trust her. He wasn't the type to make the same mistake twice and she knew that he was in her presence out of obligation and loyalty to Indie. YaYa felt so badly about the deceitful things that she had done. Chase had been nothing but loyal in the past and she had tainted his character when she had spun her web of lies.

"There is something I need to say to you, Chase," YaYa said as she sat with her feet propped up on the couch. She still wore the thin hospital gown that had been issued to her and she shivered slightly from the draftiness of the large cabin.

"You don't have to say anything to me, YaYa. Last time we were this close, just the two of us, some foul shit popped off afterward. I just want to post up and enjoy this silence until Indie arrives," he replied honestly. "I have no hard feelings, I just want to make sure there are no misunderstandings."

"I apologize for what I did to you, Chase. It was foul and I was in a really bad place. This entire beef with Leah turned me into somebody tha' I'm not," YaYa said.

She quivered.

"You're cold?" Chase asked after a beat of silence.

"Freezing and a little weak. My feet and fingers feel like they're going to fall off," she answered.

He rose to his feet and grabbed a blanket off the sofa. He wrapped it around YaYa's shoulders. "All is forgiven, YaYa," he said. "It was never needed. Now relax and get some sleep. I'm sure Indie will wake you when he arrives."

The sun crept through the curtains of the cabin and when YaYa opened her eyes, Indie sat on the floor beside her, gracing her head with loving strokes.

"You're here," she said groggily as she sat up.

"Where else would I be, ma?" he answered.

"I'm sorry," she whispered. "For every single thing I've ever done to hurt you, to betray you. I'm sorry for the lies, the pills, the power struggle—"

"I don't want to talk about any of that," he said. "When you didn't show up at the chapel yesterday I thought you'd left me, but when I found out you were in trouble I thought I had lost you. Nothing will ever make me stop loving you, Disaya, and that's on my life. You are my everything and I want to leave the past behind us and start taking steps toward a better life. I need a healthy and strong wife, baby girl. No drugs. If you ever feel the need to slip up then you come to me. I'll help you through anything and I never want you to fear another human being ever again. Leah is no longer your problem, she's mine and you know how I handle my problems. We won't talk about her anymore, she doesn't exist to you. You're a queen. You're up here," he said using his hands to show her how highly he thought of her. "Leave her down here. She dragged you down to the gutter for a while and you changed. I want my old thing back. You won't hear from her again, but you don't have to hide or watch over your shoulders this time."

"What if—"

Indie put one finger to her lips. "Don't ask questions, ma, just know that it is handled."

YaYa kissed his lips and he picked her up from the couch. "Now let's get you showered and those bandages changed, after that I'll fix you breakfast."

"Where's Chase?" she asked.

"I sent him back down to the city. There's something I need him to do."

Chapter 3

"I want this job done smooth, no fuck-ups," Chase said into the walkie-talkie as he checked his rearview mirror. The task that Indie had put on his plate was huge and there was too much at stake to drop the ball. "Trina, you back there?" he asked as he drove with one hand. He was in front of a police car that had been assigned to transport Leah from the hospital to the jail where she would await her court date. Trina was trailing the car.

"Yeah, I'm good. I'm waiting on you," she shot back confidently.

They were young and reckless. There were not many aspects to the game that they didn't feel they could conquer and taking down this transport was one of them.

"Be safe, T. If anything goes wrong you get the fuck out of here. You got me?" Chase asked.

"Nothing's going wrong. Let's snatch this damn girl and get it over with," she replied. Chase tossed the walkie-talkie in the passenger seat and then out of nowhere he slammed on the brakes suddenly. The police didn't have time to react behind him and they hit his rear at full speed, sending glass flying everywhere as his back window exploded on impact. The force of the crash pushed him forward, only for the seat belt to snatch him back. He quickly snatched the pistol from under his seat as he watched the officer that was driving get out of the car, enraged. His heartbeat increased as adrenaline pumped through his veins. *I live for this shit,* he thought as he counted the officer's steps as he approached. Indie had brought Chase into the game and taught him all that he knew, but Chase was quickly developing his own persona. He was becoming a live wire. He was about that action and loved the rush that coursed through him when it was time to put in that work. He was slowly but surely becoming a beast not only regarding his hustle, but in the muscle game as well. What had once been a young boy who got chased off the block, was now a young man who ran fifty blocks and had a love affair with aggression. With no woman, no child, or roots to slow him down he was Indie's right hand and he played the position to perfection.

"Hey what the hell do you think you're doing! You don't just put on your brakes like that! Give me your license and—"

As the police officer leaned against the window frame on the driver's side, Chase's hand came up as he placed the pistol snugly beneath the officer's chin. In an instant he saw the man's life flash in his eyes, but Chase couldn't hesitate.

Psst!

The silenced hollow tip sent the man crashing to the cement, causing his other partner much alarm. Chase pulled the rosy-cheeked Halloween mask over his face and then got out of the car. The second officer hopped out of the vehicle and positioned his body behind the open door as he aimed his gun out of the descended window. He had the perfect shield as he shouted. "Put the gun down now!" He curled his finger around the trigger preparing to squeeze but was halted by the cold kiss of Trina's gun as she placed it point-blank range against the back of his skull.

"Drop it before I put your fucking brains on the concrete," she said calmly. The cop immediately complied.

Chase ran to the back door of the police car and snatched Leah out.

"No! Please! Help!" she pleaded, screaming at the top of her lungs. She pulled away trying to make her body dead weight so that she couldn't be forced into the car easily. If she was going to get snatched in broad daylight she wasn't going to make it easy. She knew that once they took her, she was as good as dead, so she put up as much fight as she could considering that she was handcuffed and still suffering from massive injuries. Once finding out that she was under arrest, the hospital only kept her long enough to prolong her life. They released her as soon as she was well enough to be transferred to the county, but it seemed that she would never make it to a cell.

"Shut your ass up before I leave you leaking out this bitch," Chase barked as he popped the trunk to his car. He forced her inside and then looked back as he watched Trina force the second officer in the back seat. He wouldn't be able to get out. He would have to wait until someone came along to help and by then they would be long gone. She turned and nodded at Chase and then the two of them ran back to their cars, speeding away from the scene in different directions.

"Where are we going? Why are we dropping Sky off?" YaYa asked as she stood back while Indie opened her car door. The serious expression on his face worried her. She could practically see the burden sitting on his shoulders and it concerned her because she had no clue about what was troubling him.

"Sky can't go where I'm taking you," he responded. "I want to show you something."

A month had passed since the accident and she was finally up and on her feet. The fact that Indie had practically brought her back from the dead made her feel alive for the first time in years. She was herself again. Disaya Morgan . . . and it had never felt so good, but for the past few weeks Indie had been distant. The brooding look in his eyes and the clenching of his jawline caused a knot to build inside of her own chest. She had no idea what he had been plotting. The things that he had been putting in play were strictly on her behalf and today it would all unfold, he hoped flawlessly.

The city streets passed them by as they made their way to an unknown destination.

"Indie, where are you taking me?" she asked again.

"I would do anything for you and for our daughter. You know that right?" he asked her.

"Yeah, of course," she replied as she reached over and placed her hand over the one he had sitting on the gearshift. "I've never doubted that." She shifted her body so that she was facing him as curiosity wrinkled her face. "Where is this coming from?"

They pulled up to an abandoned factory and YaYa looked out of her window at the high rise. The dark windows were glassless as if someone had used them for target practice and the cement walls were tagged in graffiti. "There is something that I couldn't do for you. I will do it if you are unable to, but I knew that if you didn't witness it with your own eyes you would always have some type of doubt . . . some type of fear in your heart. I want to extinguish that."

He turned off the ignition and popped open the door as he gave her hand a gentle squeeze. "Come on," he said.

Anxiety built inside YaYa as she exited the car. She waited for him to walk around to her before she snuggled herself beneath his arm. He led her inside where Chase stood in the middle of the dimly lit room. Not even the sunshine from outside could fully illuminate the space and a chill ran through her body as she looked around trying to decipher what was hiding in the shadows.

"This way," Chase said as he led the way to a staircase and began to ascend. The only thing that could be heard was dripping pipes and the sound of their feet as they clanged up the metal stairwell. YaYa had no idea what to expect and if any other person had have brought her here she would have definitely thought she was being led to an execution, but her trust in Indie kept her calm as she followed suit.

What the hell is going on? she wondered. It wasn't long before all of her questions were answered. When she stepped out onto the rooftop and saw Leah strapped to a chair she gasped in shock.

"It ends today, ma," Indie said. "It's up to you whether you want it to be fast or slow. You don't have to do it yourself if you don't want to. If you prefer you can wait in the car and I can make this entire situation disappear for you, but I know you. You need to see it so that you don't fear it anymore. She will never be able to hurt you from where I'm sending her."

"Where's that?" YaYa whispered.

"To hell," Indie replied. He lifted YaYa's chin with his finger and stared her directly in the eyes. It was so easy to get lost in his gaze. The emotion that flowed between them in that brief moment of intimacy made her feel nothing less than unfiltered love. She and Indie had gone through plenty of ups and downs. Their story was not always perfect, but one thing she could say was that it was always pure. He would do anything for her and as she glanced over at Leah, she was reminded of how deeply his commitment to her flowed.

"How do you want to handle this?" he asked.

YaYa was at a loss for words as her mouth hung open. Her heart ached. It pained her that things had spiraled so far out of control. She yearned for normalcy where enemies ignored one another or hated each other from a distance but in her reality that would never happen. Leah's sick fixation was dangerous and it had all culminated to this moment. YaYa walked over to Leah, cautiously as if she were approaching a dangerous animal that would attack her at any moment. She took her steps one at a time, timidly, as her heart beat intensely. YaYa had been through so much at the hands of this woman. It went beyond hate, beyond shade, beyond the typical jealousy that festered in the hearts of many women. Her beef with Leah was unhealthy. Leah was mentally unstable and her insanity had slowly pulled YaYa in. Leah's legs and arms were bound so tightly to the chair she sat in that they appeared raw. There were still heavy bandages around her chest from the gunshot she was recovering from. In this state Leah should have been remorseful for all of the things she had done, but YaYa could still see the hate burning in Leah's eyes. YaYa shook her head because after all the back and forth, all the drama, the kidnapping, the single black female syndrome, all YaYa felt for Leah was pity. She was pathetic. Leah had wanted to be YaYa so badly that she had failed to see how great being Leah Richards could have been if she had given herself a chance. YaYa's life wasn't perfect. She was a whore's daughter and a pimp's honorary seed. She grew up abused . . . neglected . . . poor. She had sold her body to the highest-bidding hustler in the past. It was only Indie's love that had made her feel valued. Why Leah wanted to walk in her shoes so badly was unbeknownst. Her life wasn't shiny like a pair of new Loubs. It was worn, old, and dirty, like a pair of old gym shoes, but it was the breaking in that made it so comfortable. She had been through mud and high water to get where she was; she didn't know why Leah couldn't see that.

"Why do you hate me so much?" YaYa asked. She snatched off the tape that covered Leah's mouth so that she could receive an answer.

For the first time ever YaYa saw Leah's hard resolve soften as a tear fell down her cheek. "Because you stole my life . . . my father . . . I was supposed to be you."

Tears built in YaYa's eyes because Leah truly had no clue. Her life had not been that great. It certainly was not worth the fight that Leah had put up to take it. "This has to stop. You need help. Your mind isn't right," YaYa said, taking sympathy on her enemy. "You're sick, Leah."

"And you're weak, bitch," Leah said as she spit toward YaYa.

YaYa shook her head and began to walk away, deciding to let Indie do her dirty work. For a brief second she had considered letting him keep her life. Surely rotting in a mental hospital was better than death, but Leah couldn't leave well enough alone. Her mouth had just written herself a check that she would hate to cash. "Look at you!" Leah shouted after her. "You're pathetic! You're weak!"

YaYa turned with a look of amusement in her eyes as she walked back over to Leah. She bent directly in her face as she rested her hands on top of Leah's arms.

"I may be all of those things, Leah, but guess what? I still won. Go to hell, you evil bitch," YaYa said. She pushed Leah backward and the look of fear that took over Leah's face as her chair tipped over the edge of the building was payback for the years of torture that she had inflicted.

YaYa couldn't bring herself to look, but the ear-shattering scream caused her to close her eyes. Leah experienced ten seconds of the terror that she had made YaYa live through every day: the fear of impending death. YaYa held her breath until she heard the impact of Leah's body crashing to the cement below. "God forgive me," she whispered.

Chase walked over to the edge and peered down. "I'll clean up the mess."

Indie nodded and YaYa leaned against him as he led her away. "It's over?" she whispered in disbelief.

"It's over," he confirmed.

Chapter 4

One Year Later

YaYa had never been so high in her life. She was floating, but it was a sensation unlike anything she had ever experienced. YaYa was on cloud nine, her mental elevated to levels way above what any drug could ever provide. This was a different type of high. She was high on life. For the first time ever she had absolutely no worries. Life had a funny way of working itself out. She had endured every trial and tribulation and as she sat, staring at her reflection, she couldn't help but to become emotional. For years she had not recognized the face that looked back at her. She had been lost in a world of sex, money, chaos, lies, drugs . . . you name it, YaYa had seen it. Every moment had been consumed with thoughts of revenge, of fear, survival, but today was different. Today she knew the girl in the mirror. She was beautiful and she loved the green-eyed girl who stared back at her. No one knew exactly what she had been through, what she had survived. It had been a hard journey, but she had made it. She was the last one standing and today, Disaya Morgan felt peace.

"Are you going to cry? You better not let one tear drop! You're going to mess up your makeup," Miesha said as she quickly stood to retrieve a box of Kleenex. YaYa looked over to the young girl and smiled. They had grown close. Miesha had proved herself to the team. She had given up her freedom for YaYa and had served a hard three years in prison, without ever considering mentioning YaYa's name. She had trusted YaYa with her life and in the end she had earned her seat at YaYa's table. After placing a hefty bribe to the right judge, the case had been thrown out and Miesha was able to come home. YaYa had once thought the young girl was expendable, but after proving such loyalty, YaYa would be foolish to not show her love in return. As a result, Miesha was now family. Blood wasn't the only thing that made you related; sometimes it was your friends who showed you love the most and YaYa was forever grateful for Miesha's thoroughness. In a lot of ways Miesha reminded her of herself. Thinking about the people who surrounded her on this special day the waterworks came on full force. "Aww, YaYa," Miesha said as she grabbed a few pieces of Kleenex and dabbed at the tears that were flowing down her face.

The makeup artist working beside her chimed in, "Oh she's fine, every bride gets emotional on her wedding day. If you need to take a moment and have a nice long cry go ahead. I can always touch you up afterward. This is your day. I'm here for you," the woman said as she gave YaYa a supportive smile before turning to continue her work on Elaine.

"I'm fine," YaYa assured as she turned her eyes to the ceiling so that Miesha could blot her tears away.

Elaine turned to her with a worried expression on her face. Ever since she had met the damsel in distress, YaYa had been a complicated creature. Her son, Indie, loved her, however, and through all of the ups and downs he had stuck by her side. YaYa's was no one's idea of perfect, but somehow all of her flaws were what drew her son to this woman. "Are you really?" she asked. Elaine wanted to stay close to YaYa and nurture her to ensure that this time, she made it down the aisle. The last thing anyone wanted was for YaYa to leave Indie standing at the altar again.

YaYa confirmed with a nod. "No worries, Elaine, I'm marrying your son today. There is nothing that can stop me from becoming his wife. That man is everything to me. I am one hundred percent at peace today. I have my daughter and I have Indie, nothing can possibly go wrong," she said. She spoke with such sincerity that she brought emotion to Elaine's eyes. Everyone knew how much effort it had taken to get the couple to this point. They had endured all things that were designed to destroy them. There was plenty to celebrate today. This would be the wedding of the century.

"I am so proud of you, YaYa. You are beautiful," Elaine complimented.

YaYa reached over to give Elaine's hand a gentle squeeze before standing to retreat to her dressing room. She needed a brief moment to herself because after today, Disaya Morgan would be no more. She was about to transform into Mrs. Indie Perkins. She had never wanted anything so much in her life. Hollow nervousness filled her stomach when she saw the magnificent wedding dress hanging up on the clothes rack. Monique Lhuillier was a sight to behold in itself. The couture designer had personally been commissioned to sew every bead onto the elaborate dress. Once she stepped her curvaceous body into the design it would be nothing less than a masterpiece. Indie had wanted nothing but the finest for his bride and had given her no limits when planning the celebration. She had the best designer, the most sought-after wedding planner in New York City, and the most popular wedding venue all at her disposal. Money didn't matter. The hefty price tag was worth this one day of happiness. *Today I get to live a fairytale,* she thought as she gently touched the intricate beadwork on her gown.

Everyone who was anyone in the city was invited. YaYa didn't have many friends so the guest list was mostly Indie's friends and associates. It wasn't celebrity studded, but their red carpet was filled with all the dope boys of America. Every man who was heavy in the game was in attendance. She had no idea who half of the people were, but the turnout was well over 200 guests. Indie was well respected in his hometown so when his name was involved he brought the entire city out. The only person that YaYa wished could have been there to stand at her side was Mona. The memories of their bond played through her head like a motion picture and she sent a prayer up to the heavens in commemoration. "I do miss you, Mo," she whispered. "Who would have thought? Me in a white dress?" she cracked jokingly. "Ha! We know that's a lie!"

A knock at the door interrupted her moment and she turned to see Buchanan Slim standing before her. He was dapper as ever in a black tuxedo and he held a beaming Skylar in his arms. "Hey, handsome," YaYa greeted. She reached out for Skylar. "And hi to you too, my beautiful girl," she cooed.

"Hi, Mama," Skylar replied. She was growing so quickly that YaYa could barely keep up. The three-year-old was now walking and talking and bossing everyone around. YaYa was completely wrapped up in her role as a mother and after today, she would add wife to her resume. She looked forward to the normalcy that married life would bring. What most women thought of as a burden YaYa would take pride in. She would be her husband's house-keeper, his chef, his concubine; whatever Indie husband needed, YaYa would be it. As long as Indie made sure the streets never invaded her home again, she would make sure that she provided a safe haven whenever he walked through their door.

"You're stunning Disaya," Slim complimented. Slim hadn't always been there for her; in fact he had missed majority of her life . . . but the fact that he was standing beside her as a father should, on her wedding day, meant the world. She could sense the many regrets that burdened his shoulders. Every time he looked at her, she saw his remorse. He didn't need to speak any words of apology for YaYa to know that he was sorry. He was the only father she knew, whether it be by blood or by love . . . they were connected. Her mother had loved Slim dearly and that was reason enough for YaYa to love him too. She knew that one day they would sit down to air out the many years of unresolved issues that lay between them, but today she just wanted to be normal. She wanted to pretend that she was daddy's little girl as she clung to him while walking down the aisle toward the man she loved.

"Thanks, Slim," she replied.

"I'm going to take this little flower girl to the front while you get dressed. I just wanted to stop in and tell you that I love you. Dynasty would be proud. You are the type of woman that she always wanted to become," he said. He stared off into space momentarily and YaYa knew that he was consumed by the memory of her mother.

Miesha and Elaine slipped into the room just as Slim made his exit. "It's time to get you into your dress. Indie's all ready for you and your guests are seated. It's time to begin," Elaine said.

YaYa nodded. "Okay, I'm on my way out. Just give me a few more minutes." When she was alone YaYa she dropped to her knees. After all that she had survived she was extremely humbled and grateful for this moment. She had never thought she would find a man like Indie, let alone become his wife. It was as if God had designed them uniquely for each other and no one else. Indie was a gift and she would be forever thankful for his presence in her present.

"God, thank you for seeing me through. I am forever a work in progress, but I love you for loving me through all of my imperfections. When I'm burdened and weak you give me strength. When I'm happy you tap my shoulder in remembrance of humility. It is only because of you that I have made it this far. Thank you for this day. Amen," she prayed. The door opened once more and Elaine peeked her head inside.

"Baby, you have an entire ballroom of people waiting on you, not to mention a very nervous groom. If you don't get out there soon he may run away on you this time," Elaine joked. "You ready to get dressed now?"

YaYa nodded as she wiped away the single tear that slid down her cheek. "I'm ready," she replied with a huge sigh. She was so nervous that it felt as if she had anvils sitting on her chest. Her anxiety was so overwhelming that she could barely breathe.

Elaine chuckled, recognizing the familiar case of cold feet that every bride experienced. "It'll pass," she reassured. "Just keep breathing and keep walking until you see your man. When you lay eyes on him, if the feeling is still there you run for the door, but if it melts away like snow on a sunny morning then you know that he's the one," she schooled. It was the same words that her own mother had told her years ago the day she got married. YaYa nodded as Elaine helped her shimmy herself into her wedding dress. She walked to the full-length mirror and held her hands out to her sides as she pivoted on her tiptoes to see all the angles of the dress. "Do I look okay?"

Elaine had to cover her mouth to keep from letting the sob of emotion creep out. She blinked away tears while nodding her head. "He's going to love you," Elaine whispered as she placed the sheer veil gently in YaYa's hair.

YaYa exhaled as she placed her hands on her stomach in an attempt to still the fluttering inside. She beamed a wide smile of excitement. The beautiful silk gown hugged her body until it overflowed with silk ruffles at the bottom. The mermaid-style gown was flawless and for that one moment YaYa had no insecurities. She felt simply stunning as she rushed out of the room, the long train trailing behind her.

Their wedding party was intimate. No distant cousins or long-lost friends stood at their altar. They only wanted their immediate circle beside them as they exchanged vows. With Trina missing in action in Houston, Miesha was her only bridesmaid. Chase the only groomsman. The wedding party focused on simplicity but the wedding itself was nothing short of grand. YaYa stood behind the double doors of the St. Regis as she waited for her cue to walk. Most brides had a fleeting moment just before they wed where they second-guessed their decision, but YaYa was certain. In her heart of hearts she knew that the man waiting for her at the front of the beautiful banquet hall was whom she was meant to be with. So when the doors finally opened, all of her anxiety dissipated, just as Elaine said it would. She had no doubts about the man that she had chosen. The beautiful sound of the four violinists resounded in the air as their strings hummed the subtle tune of "Canon in D" and YaYa graced the aisle. Gasps filled the air as the guests took her in, but YaYa didn't see anyone but Indie. He stood, dapper as ever, in a grey Tom Ford tuxedo. His hair freshly cut and lined, his hands folded in front of his body, posture strong. He was her destination and the look of certainty in his eyes made her even more confident. Each graceful step she took brought her closer to her destiny. She walked down the aisle but it was as if her feet weren't touching the floor. She was floating. It was that high feeling again. She was floating and nothing could bring her down off of that cloud. She clung to Slim as he held her securely as he patted her hand, being the support system that she had always needed.

In her head she wondered if she was good enough for this man. Since meeting him he had always come to her rescue. She was ready to give her entire heart to him because he was worthy, but was she? Did she deserve Indie? A part of her didn't think so. After all that she had taken him through, all of the times she had disappointed him, betrayed him, he could have easily found a better match, but he loved her all the same. She was the yin and he, her yang. He was the shrimp to her grits, the rhythm to her flow; he was the element in her life that made things complete. They were just right together. He was the love of her life but above that he was her protector. With Indie, she felt . . .

Safe.

Secure.

He had promised to never let anyone hurt her again and it had taken her awhile to get to this place but she finally believed him.

She saw him standing tall, biting his inner cheek as his jaw muscle tensed. His eyes were misted as he fought off emotion. His love for her was literally pouring out of his soul. Indie had never been a weak man and the fact that he could barely keep his composure let her know that this love thing that they shared was real. There had never been another bond that was more authentic. As soon as she made it to him, Slim shook Indie's hand and returned to his seat as the couple stood before the crowded room.

YaYa's smile was too radiant, her face too angelic. Her presence was too overwhelming for Indie to just stand there, so instead, he acted on his emotions and pulled her in for a kiss. The entire room erupted in applause and fanfare as YaYa grabbed the sides of his face and returned his affection with passion.

"You're beautiful, ma, so beautiful," he whispered in her ear. They were a young couple in deep love and it was visible to even the blindest of eyes. The pastor cleared his throat and smiled down at the couple.

"As we can see there is an abundance of love in the building today," he began. "We are all present to witness this man and this woman as they become one in the eyes of our Heavenly Father."

YaYa was so lost in Indie's stare that she barely heard a word that was spoken. The sound of her own heart beating deafened her and all she could feel was bliss. It was as if some invisible happy fairy was sprinkling joy dust all over her. She tingled it felt so good. Suddenly she felt a tug at the bottom of her dress and the crowd laughed slightly. She looked down to see Skylar. Her precious child was a perfect blend of her parents. YaYa bent down to pick up the only palpable evidence of their love.

"Hey, baby girl," she whispered. "Mommy is marrying Daddy. I need you to be a good girl," she said.

"I want to marry daddy too," Skylar replied. YaYa laughed along with the guests and when Elaine stood to take Sky back to her seat, YaYa shook her head. "She can stay. She's right where she belongs."

"Let's cut to the chase, Rev," Indie said with a wink. "Li'l mama won't be this calm too much longer."

The pastor nodded and said, "Disaya, please repeat after me. I, Disaya . . ."

YaYa listened carefully as she recited her vows, genuinely meaning every word, but before she could even finish the clanging of the double doors drew her attention. Everyone turned as a dark-skinned woman entered the ballroom.

"Wait! Wait! Please stop! This wedding can not happen!" she yelled.

YaYa's heart crashed into her stomach as confusion replaced the happiness on her face.

"Parker?" Indie gasped as he released YaYa's hand and his eyes widened in shock. A feeling of sickness invaded YaYa when she saw the spark of familiarity ring in Indie's gaze. She sat her daughter down on the floor and gave her a gentle pat on the bottom as she whispered, "Go to Grandma Elaine." She stood upright and turned to Indie as anger caused her to tremble. "You know her?" YaYa asked accusingly, equally stunned.

"Please, Indie, you can't marry her," the woman said desperately as she came closer to the altar. "You know that when she came down the aisle to you, all you could see was me."

"Indie, who the fuck is she?" YaYa demanded, completely losing her couth. The crowd was silent but clearly tuned in as every eye in the building stared at Indie and then at YaYa and then at the mystery intruder who had the moxie to bust up a wedding ceremony. Things like this only happened in the movies. No one could believe that this scene was playing out in front of them. It was a recipe for drama and YaYa's fuse was undoubtedly lit. All that growth and maturity that she had just acknowledged in the dressing room was slowly dwindling. She wanted to revert back to her roots and drag this bitch for having the audacity to ruin her day. The ballroom was so silent you could hear a pin drop as everyone waited for Indie's response.

Indie stood there stuck between a rock and a hard place. He was at a loss for words. Never in a million years had he ever thought he would see her face again. Parker Banks, the first woman who had ever broken his heart was now standing in front of him, on his wedding day at that, asking him to call everything off. There had been a time when he would have obliged her request without hesitation. He hadn't seen her in years, but here she stood, looking as beautiful as she had the day she walked out of his apartment eight years before. It was as if she hadn't aged at all. She had always possessed an innocence that drove him crazy and as he stood between his past and his future he couldn't deny the slight tug that she had on his heart.

"You need to leave," Indie said as he began to turn back to his bride. He turned to Chase who stood as his best man, behind him. The last thing he wanted to do was ruin this day for YaYa. She deserved this. He had committed to her. He couldn't look back to Parker. "Get rid of her."

"You can't get rid of me, Indie, I have your child and you are not marrying anyone before you hear me out," she said as tears began to shine in her eyes. "Please, Indie, I love you, I always have and you know deep down that you've always wanted to hear me say that," she pleaded, unashamed and brazen.

Disaya's mouth fell open and she doubled over in real physical pain. It felt as if someone had deflated her. It was like the air had been punched out of her lungs. "I knew this was too good to be true. This day was too perfect to ever belong to me," she whispered.

She stood to her feet as Indie looked back and forth between her and this girl who had shown up out of nowhere. YaYa didn't need to see any more. He was indecisive and his hesitation was enough to let her know that he was unsure. He didn't have to say anything; his actions told it all. "You don't know who to pick," YaYa whispered, as the ultimate hurt entered her. The fact that she saw confusion in his eyes was enough to let her know that the nuptials were over. Love may have been many things, but it was never uncertain.

"YaYa . . . baby girl, just give me a minute," he whispered, a pained look in his eyes. "I need to speak to her."

YaYa shook her head in disgust. "A minute?" she huffed in disbelief. "How about a lifetime. You can have that." She stormed past Indie, a vision of white as she held up the fabric of her dress as she ran down the aisle in tears.

"YaYa!"

The crowd gasped as she went racing toward the exit.

"I've got her," Chase said as he went tailing after her.

Indie watched helplessly as YaYa went running out of his life. He wanted to go after her, but this ghost who had walked back into his life had him stuck. He walked up to Parker and grabbed her roughly by her elbow as he dragged her out of the room, using a side door. Chatter immediately erupted as soon as the groom disappeared and Elaine instantly rose out of her seat.

"Ladies and gentlemen, thank you for your presence but as you just witnessed there will not be a wedding taking place today," she said. She turned to Bill, her husband, with a worried look on her face as the guest departed. She didn't know exactly what this meant, but she was sure that Indie and YaYa couldn't sustain a blow this big. This would undoubtedly be the straw that broke the camel's back and ended their relationship for good.

YaYa burst out of the prestigious hotel and onto the busy streets of NYC. Her tear-stained faced alarmed a few pedestrians as she bent over in anguish. She looked right, then left, but none of those paths allowed her to escape quickly enough.

"YaYa!"

She turned back to see Chase and more disappointment filled her. Indie hadn't even come after her. *He's still in there . . . with her,* YaYa thought. She shook her head and turned around to see a pearl-tinted Infiniti truck as it pulled up in front of the hotel. She didn't hesitate. She opened the door and stuffed her dress inside.

"Yo, ma, what the—"

"I don't know who you are, but please just get me out of here," she whispered.

The man looked out of his window at Chase who stood baffled as he lifted his hands as if to say, "What the fuck?"

He assessed the situation within seconds. He didn't know what had caused this stunning bride to abandon her groom, but the heartbroken expression on her face was enough for him to put the car in drive and ease away from the curb.

YaYa looked in the side mirror and saw Chase kick at the air in frustration. She couldn't contain the sobs that wrecked her.

She didn't care that she was in a stranger's car or that she had no idea where she was going. This cry just needed to get out because the pain she was harboring was too great to contain.

"Look, ma, I don't know what to say here. I'll take you wherever you need to go, but you've got to let me know what's up. I'm driving in circles here," he said with sympathy.

She shook her head and closed her eyes unable to calm her emotions.

"At least tell me your name," he pushed.

"YaYa," she whispered. "My name is YaYa."

"Under normal circumstances I'd say it's nice to meet you," he replied. "But it doesn't seem appropriate. I'm lost here, baby girl. Is there somewhere I can take you?"

He reached in his breast pocket and passed her a pocket square. YaYa graciously accepted. "I'm so sorry. You don't know me. You can drop me off on the next block. I'll catch a cab from there. You must think I'm insane."

"I'm not dropping you off in the middle of New York City. I'll take you wherever you need me to. I don't think you're crazy, sweetheart. I think a nigga broke your heart and for that I think he must be the crazy one," he answered honestly.

YaYa's eyes met his, shocked by his kind words. The man kept his eyes focused on the road and for the first time she took him in. He was clad in tailored Ferragamo. His skin was dark as the finest chocolate. He was handsome and the five o'clock shadow he rocked was lined perfectly. His facial expression was stern, serious, and unrevealing. YaYa immediately noticed the qualities of a made man. The expensive watch he wore rested on a tattoo-covered wrist. He was so dark that his ink barely showed. His jawline was strong, his posture confident, the look in his eyes determined. He was a boss and at that moment YaYa was so grateful to fate for sending him to her, even if it was only to act as her getaway driver.

"I don't have anywhere to go. I can't go home right now. I don't have any money on me, but I do have money. If you could let me borrow a few hundred dollars so that I can get a room, I swear to God I'll pay you back for the inconvenience."

The man chuckled slightly and gave her a small smile. "Don't worry about it, ma, I don't need no paybacks. I think I can manage," he said in amusement.

Suddenly curious about who he was and why he was being so generous, YaYa asked, "Who are you? Most people would expect something in return."

"My name's Ethic and I'm certainly not most people. Now dry your pretty eyes, ma, I'll take you somewhere where you can clear your head and rest up."

Chapter 5

The black trails that ran down her cheek revealed her misery and YaYa shook her head in disgrace as she ran hot water over the hotel's towel. She wiped away her makeup knowing that if she didn't it would only run with her tears. She was an emotional wreck.

Knock. Knock.

She turned and opened the bathroom door. "I brought you some food and a change of clothes, you look like you're about a size eight," Ethic said.

She gave him a half-hearted smile and replied, "You're incredibly nice, thank you so much for"—she paused for a beat—"sticking around."

"It's nothing, really. I'm glad I could help. If my daughter was in your shoes, I'd want someone to do the same," he said politely. "I paid for two nights and my card is on file so you can order food and whatever else you need. That should give you enough time to clear your head before going home. I'm sorry this day didn't go like you would have wanted it to. You would have made a beautiful bride, ma."

The gentle way in which he spoke to YaYa melted her, bringing tears to her eyes. She was holed up, hiding out of embarrassment from her fiancé. The last thing she wanted to do was be alone.

"Ethic?" she called after him just as he reached the door to the suite.

"Can you stay?" she asked. "I mean . . ." She cleared her throat. "I could really use the company right now."

Ethic checked his watch and YaYa could sense that she was holding him up. "I'm sorry," she said. "You don't even know me. You don't have time for this type of crazy. Please go. I'm fine."

He paused as he stared at her sympathetically. YaYa shook her head and led him toward the door. "I'm okay, I promise," she assured. "You've done more than enough. As long as you don't mind me ordering a bottle of the best champagne to celebrate my non-union," she shot sarcastically, giving him her best smile. Although she was trying her hardest to convince Ethic, he wasn't buying her act.

"I know this doesn't mean much coming from a stranger, but the nigga who left you like this on your wedding day isn't a very smart man," he said. He leaned down and kissed her cheek before making his exit.

"What the fuck was that?" Indie yelled as he forced Parker into his hotel suite. "I haven't seen you in eight years, P, and you march your pretty ass in on my wedding day and blow up the joint?" He was furious and confused as he pinched the bridge of his nose while bowing his disgraced head.

"You still think I'm pretty, huh?" Parker said with a slight smile.

"Don't start that shit with me, Parker. This isn't a game. Do you know what you just did?" he asked. He walked over to the bar and poured himself a glass of cognac.

"I do know, Indie. I stopped the love of my life from marrying someone else. You don't belong with her, Indie. You're mine and you've always been mine," she said. "We have a child."

"What?" Indie shot in confusion.

A knock at the door interrupted the conversation as Elaine peeked her head inside. She held baby Skylar in her arms.

"Great," Parker said as threw up her arms, exasperated. Elaine had never been her biggest fan.

"I'm sorry to interrupt . . ."

"Sure you are," Parker mumbled under her breath.

Elaine cut her eyes at Parker giving her a cold stare before turning to Indie. "You need to go find YaYa, son," she said. "I can handle this situation. Go find her now."

"Indie, I came to speak with you not your mother," Parker insisted.

Indecision danced through him. He didn't know what to do. His past and his future were playing tug of war with his heart. How could he not want to hear Parker out? He had loved her for such a long time. If she indeed had given birth to his child she deserved his full attention as she explained herself. On the other hand, YaYa was his present and his future wrapped into one. Now he was being forced to choose between them. "I have to go. I'll be back. Don't go anywhere," Indie said sternly. He turned to Chase who had entered the room. "See to it that she doesn't."

He nodded as Indie rushed to find his bride.

"Chase, would you take the baby downstairs and get her some food? She has to be starving by now," Elaine said. "All of that reception food shouldn't go to waste. Fix her a plate and if there are any guests still here, tell them they are welcome to eat before going home."

He hesitated as he looked at Parker.

"I've got this," Elaine guaranteed.

Chase took Sky from the room and once the two women were alone she turned to Parker.

"You clean up well," Elaine said with tight lips as she took the young woman in. She had always been a beautiful girl. Her ebony skin was smooth like silk and held not one mark or scar. Her hair was big as her natural curls framed her lovely face. Her eyes were a shade of brown so light that they seemed mystical, as if she had the power to read straight through bullshit. She huffed as she stared Elaine down with a bent brow of disdain. The Chanel bag she carried to accessorize her Yves Saint Laurent pencil skirt and high-crop sweater was statement enough. Parker had arrived and she wasn't leaving anytime soon; at least not until she had gotten what she had come back for.

"Same old Elaine," Parker scoffed as she crossed her arms.

"What are you doing here?" Elaine spewed nastily through clenched teeth. "I paid you good money to stay away from my son."

"Yeah, well twenty thousand dollars wasn't enough to keep me away when my child started asking me why all of the other boys on his basketball team have dads but he doesn't," Parker shot back while fighting back emotion. She cleared her throat and squared her shoulders. "Your money won't get rid of me this time. I was young and easily manipulated back then. I'm a grown woman now and my son deserves to know his father. You and I both know that if I had stayed in New York, he would be married to me. We were supposed to be a family and I realize that now. So no matter what you say or do, I'm not leaving town until I explain myself to him and once he hears the entire story, the *true* story, we both know that he'll come running back to me . . . where he belongs."

Parker stormed past Elaine bumping her shoulder on the way out and leaving Elaine speechless. Elaine was so shaken that she had to reach out to hold the chair in front of her to steady herself. Her hand covered her mouth as she slowly lowered herself to a seated position. Before to-day she hadn't thought about Parker in quite some time. In fact, ever since Indie had brought YaYa to her house, she had not given Parker a second thought, but now it seemed that her house of lies was about to come crashing to the ground. As she scrolled through her memory she reevaluated the decisions that she had made eight years ago. She knew that nothing could stay hidden forever and the truth was about to come to light. Elaine only hoped that Indie would understand, but as she thought back on the things she had done she already knew that her son would never forgive her. Her sins were just too great.

Chapter 6

Parker and Indie's past

"This is some bullshit," Parker mumbled as she stuffed her hands into the pockets of her down coat. The holes that were in the pockets did little to provide warmth, but it was better than letting the freezing elements bite at her delicate hands. New York's winters were brutal and Parker was at its mercy as she made her way to her evening job. The book bag she wore on her back slowed her down as she made her way through the slush and dirty snow. The eleven blocks from her Queens apartment to the dingy hotel where she worked nights felt like a marathon on nights like this. It seemed as though she would never arrive. She made it a minute before her shift began and she clocked in right before the clock struck 12:01 a.m.

"Cutting it kind of close there, girl," Big Jim, the manager, said as he sat eyeing her with a scowl of irritation. She was usually half an hour early, which allowed Big Jim to leave ahead of schedule and spin the block, trolling for his evening blowjob before he made his way home to his naïve wife.

"I'm right on time," she replied in a sing-song voice as she maneuvered around the forty-something overweight white man. Her boss was a real ass, but he was the only person who had given her a real job. She had been working for him ever since her freshman year *way before she was even legal to work. He had paid her under the table. $200 per week. It wasn't much but to Parker it was everything. It kept clothes on her back and food in her stomach during hard times. She lived in a household with three sisters, all older, and a mother who had bore them so young that she seemed like a fourth sibling. In her home everybody fended for self. Each one of her sisters had learned that their well-being was their own responsibility. As Parker watched her mother rotate men in and out of her bedroom just to make ends meet, Parker knew that it wasn't an option for her. So instead of tricking with the older dudes on her block, or manipulating men for money like her sisters, she got a gig. From midnight to 6:00 a.m. she worked six nights a week, only to get dressed in one of the vacant hotel rooms and report to school by 7:45 sharp. She spent more time at the sleazy hotel than she did in her own house. Yes, it was low paying, and yes, she was tired all the time, but it was an honest job and she didn't have to lie on her back or beg a nigga to throw her cash when she needed something. That alone made the job worth it.*

"What happened to eleven-thirty, toots?" Big Jim fussed.

"You don't pay me to get here at eleven-thirty. You pay me to be here at midnight. I'm here. Good night, Big Jim," she said. Big Jim mumbled his complaints as he walked out of the door, leaving Parker to man the hotel alone.

She pulled out her schoolbooks and opened them up as she began to do her homework. It wasn't long before the words turned into a blur before her and she fell asleep right at the front desk.

"Yo, shorty," she heard as a knock on the desk caused her to pop up in surprise. Her eyes shot to the clock and then at the face of the group of people in front of

her. *"You sleeping on the job and shit,"* the guy said as he stood with his arm draped around a pretty girl in a short skirt and stiletto heels. *"You got a little slob on your cheek, shorty."*

The girl and the group of people behind him laughed at her expense. This wasn't unusual. They were the beautiful people. They were the hustlers and the fly girls of the block with their designer clothes and flashy cars. She wouldn't doubt that they bled gold if someone told her so. She saw how they blew through money like it was nothing and while her sisters desperately chased after those types of dudes, she avoided them like the plague. Parker knew that there was a cost to pay to be on the arms of a hustler. She saw it day in and day out in her neighborhood. A nigga could take the prettiest girl on the block and make her a hood star overnight, only to toss her to the side when he was done and move on to the next. Parker had told herself that it would never happen to her, which was easier said than done because niggas wasn't checking for her like that. She wasn't a hot commodity yet. Her style wasn't in. Her clothes weren't marked with multiple labels nor her face drew on like a clown and she definitely refused to burn her fingers every day trying to straighten the messy curls of her hair. The most that she wore was a coat of lip gloss and a few swipes of mascara, the rest of that shit was for the birds. She wasn't fishing and she wasn't using herself as bait so she was often overlooked despite the fact that she was nothing but purely beautiful.

"You're a funny guy," she replied. *"You want a room or not?"*

"Yeah, yeah, give me two rooms, sleeping beauty," the guy cracked. He was full of jokes and the girls who were hanging off of his every word found him most amusing.

"Leave the girl alone, Bay," one of the other guys said as he ended his call on his cell phone. He stepped to the front desk and pulled out a large knot of cash. "How much we owe you?"

"Two hundred dollars," she said. He slid the money across the counter and noticed the books she was reading.

"You're in college or something?" he asked.

"High school," she said.

He looked at the clock and frowned. "It's two in the morning, ma. What's a high school student doing working this late?

"I don't have the luxury to sleep. It's school and work, work and school. If I don't work I don't eat today, if I don't finish school I don't eat tomorrow. So I do both to make sure I don't ever starve," she replied.

The guy smiled. "I never heard a chick talk like that, shorty. You got something going on up here," he said as he pointed to his own temple. "That's real dope."

"Yo, what the fuck, bro? Get the keys and let's go. You and shorty blowing my vibe," Bay said as he now had his arms draped around not only his girl, but the other one as well.

Parker handed him the room keys. "You're all set," she said.

"Thanks, shorty," he replied. He pointed to the books as he backpedaled away from the desk. "Get back to it." He gave her a wink and she smiled a rare smile as she watched him walk down the hall. She looked at the copy of his license that she had made and read his name: "Indie Perkins."

The memory of Parker's first encounter with Indie caused her lips to turn up in a faint smile. She remembered it like it was yesterday. The baggy clothes, the cocky attitude he possessed . . . She had thought he was a typical d-boy but he had quickly shown her otherwise.

She walked into the ballroom where Indie's wedding had taken place. It was beautiful and as she looked around tears accumulated in her eyes. He had spared no expense. Every single decoration was arranged perfectly, down to the Swarovski crystals that hung from the ceilings, making it feel as if the room sparkled. A piece of her felt guilty that she had interrupted such a lavish ceremony, but the part of her that thought of Indie every single day had pushed her to go and get her man. Not a day had gone by since Elaine had chased her out of town, that she didn't miss Indie. He consumed her thoughts and when she closed her eyes it was him who met her in her dreams. She had tried the dating thing and had even gotten a few marriage proposals, but whenever things got too serious with anyone, Parker cut it short. The heart wants what the heart wants and hers had always wanted Indie Perkins. She hated the fact that he had obviously moved on, but she had faith that the love that they shared was not one-sided. She knew what Indie felt for her. It had been so strong back in the day that she was confident that once the shock of her reemergence wore off, he would realize that those same feelings were still inside of him. For Parker the love had never gone dormant, it was very much alive and when she saw him standing at the top of the aisle with another woman, she knew . . . she knew that she wasn't leaving New York without him.

Parker made her way to the front of the ballroom but was shocked to find Indie sitting with his head bowed in the front row.

"I'm probably the last person you want to see," she said. She noticed the cell phone that he gripped tightly in his hands. "She isn't taking your call?" She was sympathetic to Indie's plight. The last thing she wanted to do was hurt him, but she couldn't let him go through with the wedding, not before giving her a chance to explain.

If he wanted to marry someone else after she spoke with him then fine, but today . . . today no nuptials were going down. She didn't mean to be a bitch, but she only got one shot at life and she desperately wanted a love like Indie in hers.

Indie looked at her in frustration and then confusion. "I waited for you for four years, Parker. I put my shit on hold for you, froze off my heart but you never came back. You didn't call, write, text, none of that and on the day that I'm supposed to marry my girl you show up . . ."

"I saw the announcement in the paper and it broke my heart," she admitted. "I don't want you to make a vow to God to love anyone other than me. We were supposed to be forever," she said.

"Yeah, until you blew town," he shot back as he shook his head from side to side. "Now it's too late. I'm with somebody."

"I didn't just blow town, Indie. Your mother paid me to leave because I was pregnant. We have a son. He's seven," Parker revealed.

She had envisioned this moment for years. She had wondered how Indie would react, if he would be angry . . . but in all the ways that she had imagined this going down she never expected to see utter devastation on his face. Her nerves danced frantically as she fiddled with her fingers anxiously.

"Indie, say something," she whispered.

"Where is he? This kid that you claim belongs to me?" he asked.

She raised an eyebrow defensively but decided not to challenge his crass statement. He had a right to be upset. She would give him that one, he wouldn't get another though. "He's in DC with my mom."

"You kept my child a secret all this time?" he asked, this time silent as the enormity of the situation sunk in. How could he have a kid in the world that he knew nothing about? "What do you mean my mother paid you? Why would she . . ." He paused as he stood to his feet while staring intently at her, brow dipped in angst. "Why would you do this to me? How could you keep this from me? We were—"

"So in love," Parker finished for him. "I'm still so in love, Indie. I've always been, but your mother, she . . . she . . . she made me think . . ." Parker couldn't find the words to accurately describe how it all had gone down. "I was young and afraid and she offered me an out. I took twenty thousand dollars to disappear. I was supposed to use some of the money to get an abortion, but I couldn't. When I laid down on that table all I kept seeing was you. I took the money but I could not kill anything that was a part of you," she whispered. Tears glistened as she spoke. Emotions that she had kept hidden for years were now spilling out of her as she spoke. There had been so many hard times as a single mother that she had lost count. "I wanted to call you so many times, but after the first year passed I didn't know how . . . but I'm here now and I miss you, Indie."

He was silent but the hurt that consumed him was palpable. Parker could practically hear his heart splitting in two. He rubbed the top of his head, overwhelmed, and she knew that he needed reprieve. She had spoken her truth and standing in front of him awaiting an answer only added pressure to him. "I'm staying at The London in Manhattan," she said. "I'll be here for a week. If I don't hear from you by then I'll know that you want nothing to do with me."

As badly as she wanted to reach out and kiss him she knew that it wasn't the time. She began to make her exit.

"P," Indie called.

She turned.

"Are you okay? Do you need anything . . . money or anything?" he asked.

She smiled and shook her head. "No, Indie, I'm not here to take anything from you. This little ghetto girl turned out just fine. I teach Women's Studies at Howard U in DC. I recently got an offer to teach here in the city. I couldn't see myself coming back here without reaching out to you. I'm not here for your money. I don't need it. I do need you, however, our son needs you and I miss everything about the love we used to share. If you miss it too I'll see you before the week's end."

She walked out and exhaled in relief. She had just faced her biggest challenge or so she thought. She had no idea that the woman in Indie's life would put up one hell of a fight. This was about to be a tug of war that would only end up splitting Indie's heart in half.

Chapter 7

The meeting that Ethic had was a once-in-a-lifetime opportunity, but he couldn't help but to be distracted as he made his way back to the hotel. It had been a hell of a day, and being the getaway car for a runaway bride, a beautiful one at that, had thrown his plans all the way off. It had been seven years since he had thought of stepping his foot back into the game. After losing a woman he loved dearly to domestic violence, he had removed himself from the street life completely. He had two beautiful girls to raise back home and knew that he had to tread carefully to make sure that his actions didn't affect their safety. He hadn't touched a brick in years, but he had never lost the knack of the hustle. If Ethic had stayed in the ring there was no doubt that he would be moving heavy weight. His name still rang bells all throughout the Midwest. As a young kid he had earned a decades worth of respect and a lifetime's worth of dough, but now at thirty-two he was just trying to keep his head low and his nose clean. He had made smart investments in stocks and bonds that had nearly quadrupled his "safe" money. Now he was a legit businessman. The owner of a trucking company that had government contracts to transport auto parts for the big three automakers in the Midwest. He employed over one hundred people and although it didn't give him the same rush as his days of flipping keys, it gave him security and a peace of mind that money could not buy. He never wanted to survive another tragedy. Watching a woman whom he loved, who he shared his bed with, be gunned down by another man all because of him, had been too hard. He had walked away from the streets that same day and never looked back. But when he received a phone call from one of the legends in the game requesting his presence, he could not say no. The fact that he even had to reschedule the meeting after YaYa had jumped in his car was risking the connection, but he had to admit that meeting her had been worth it. She was a beautiful girl and their chance encounter had left him curious. Despite the fact that he knew nothing about her, he wondered if she was okay. He gave his keys to the valet and then made his way to the luxury restaurant in the lobby of the five-star hotel.

His eyes traced the perimeter of the establishment, an old habit from his illegitimate days, as he gave the maître d' his name. He had no idea who to expect or what would go down from here but he was prepared for anything. When someone of this magnitude requested your presence, the outcome was usually profitable or detrimental . . . it could swing either way. He was escorted to an obscure area in the back. There was a wall that separated this one table from the rest of the room. Two men stood as a buffer between him and a beautiful woman who was sitting comfortably with a napkin folded in her lap. Her long hair was jet-black and bone straight with a simple part down the middle of her head. The curves of the black slip dress she wore were just as dangerous as the look in her eyes. She was beautiful and poisonous all at the same time. *Damn,* he thought as he took a step forward. He was halted by the firm hand of one of the men. Ethic understood the notion of bodyguards but he didn't respect their gangster. He didn't give two fucks about whom they were protecting. You needed permission to lay hands on him. He recognized Zya as a boss, but what she didn't realize was she was in the presence of one as well. Mutual respect was a must. He quickly grabbed the man's wrist firmly, applying pressure to the sensitive space between the bones of his hand and arm.

"I'm not a little nigga. You don't lay hands on me. We understand each other?" he asked. The other bodyguard went to move but the girl put her hand up to stop the chaos before it erupted. Ethic released the bodyguard and met eyes with the woman in front of him.

"I see everything I've heard about you is correct," she said with a small smirk and a look of interest in her eyes. "Do you know who I am?" she asked. The question wasn't cocky and she wasn't trying to grandstand. He could tell that she was trying to see how much he knew about her.

"I've heard some things about the infamous Zya Miller," he replied.

"Believe only half of them," she said with a small laugh. "Someone in my position can never be too careful, Ezra," she said, using his legal first name, which let him know she had done her research. "My men mean no disrespect. They are just cautious. I pay them good money to be. If you don't mind, I'd like to make sure that my safety and freedom isn't in jeopardy." She stood to her feet. "May I?"

She stepped closely to Ethic and the scent of her Dior perfume immediately enveloped him as she placed her hand on his chest.

"I'm not wired, ma," he said. "There's a pistol on my hip, but do you really think I'm going to pop off in a crowded restaurant?"

The woman's hands moved across his strong chest, she wrapped her arms around his broad shoulders and down his back, feeling every muscle that he worked so hard to maintain. They were standing so close that he could smell the mint on her breath. She brought her hands around his waistline and removed the gun, expertly removing the clip without ever breaking their intense stare. She placed the now useless weapon back in Ethic's waist holster. He smiled, because every rumor that he had ever heard fit her to a T. "You satisfied yet?" he asked.

"It takes so much more than that to satisfy me," she replied as she blushed slightly before taking two steps back. She extended her hand. "Please have a seat."

Ethic sat and she immediately changed the tone to straight business. "I have a tendency to keep my ear to the street," she said. "A partner of mine told me that Benjamin Atkins used to run a little city by the name of Flint, MI. He said that more money was made on those streets than in Detroit, New York, Atlanta . . . so you know that piqued my curiosity. So I kept digging and I found out that it wasn't Benjamin Atkins that was flooding the streets. It was his connect . . . you. While it was relatively easy to find out information on Benjamin, it was almost impossible to find a back story on you. All I know is that you fell in love with Atkins's daughter and that she was gunned down in your car almost seven years ago. You haven't touched dope since that day. Not a zip, not an ounce, not a ki' . . . You've been like a ghost to the streets ever since," she concluded. "Why is that?"

Ethic felt a stir of emotion as she took him down an unpleasant stroll down memory lane. Those had been some of the worst days of his life. "It's not something I like to discuss. The past is behind me for a reason. I don't live that way anymore."

"What's the story? The quintessential thug finds God? Has remorse? Did you turn to Allah?" Zya pried.

"I realized that no amount of money was worth the life of someone I loved. I lost someone very special to me, you know that, but you don't know the children who are depending on me. I have a little girl who likes ballet. She wants her daddy in the audience at every recital." He paused for a beat to gather himself before continuing,

"You don't know the younger sister that my dead girl-friend left behind or my little boy who wants to grow up to be just like me. I watched doctors cut my son from his dead mother's stomach behind this game. I was left to raise all three of them on my own. I am all they have so I had to make a choice. I could either be a street legend or a legend in their eyes; I chose the latter."

"That's commendable," Zya said with a look of admiration in her eyes. She wished that she could leave it all alone. "To walk away from the allure of it all is—"

"It was hard, but I didn't have a choice," Ethic interrupted. "So I'm not quite sure what I'm doing here, sitting in front of Ms. La Cosa Nostra herself. You move weight—"

"And you have the means to move weight across state lines," Zya finished for him, ending the guessing games. "There will be no risk to you. All you have to do is pick up and deliver."

"There is always a risk and I don't need the money," he said.

"No, but you miss the thrill . . . you miss the ride, Ethic. I can see it in your eyes. You lived this life for so long. You had so much power. I understand the need to take a break and clear your head. You've been through a lot, but we both know that eventually you'll want back in, so why fight the inevitable. Plus I've got a hundred racks for every shipment you move successfully."

"You can get anyone for this. There are thousands of companies," he said.

"But there is only one you. I know your track record. You're one of the biggest connects out of the Midwest. Or at least you used to be. I only work with thorough people. People who know the business," she said. "So do we have a deal?"

Ethic shook his head, still playing hardball.

"Maybe this will help sway your decision," she said. She pulled out a manila folder from the handbag that sat at her feet and slid it across the table.

Still images lay inside and when Ethic peered at the photos pure rage flared in his eyes. It was like putting gasoline on a fire as he stared at the old enemy. Mizan. The man who had caused the death of Raven Atkins. She had been the mother of Ethic's son, and the woman he loved most in the world and her killer was staring back at him through the photo. "If you say yes to this deal, I'll give you his location. That is the man who killed Raven right? The same man who put that scar on your face when he tried to blow you up in a car? He was also behind the setup of your old friend, Raven's father, Benny Atkins. He slipped through your hands when you tried to get your revenge and you haven't been able to find him since."

Ethic looked at her in shock. She truly was a woman who believed in doing her homework. Ethic hadn't spoken Raven's name in years to avoid the weak pit that formed in his stomach when he heard it. He pinched the tip of his nose as he sniffed to contain his emotions. "I'm in," Ethic said without hesitation. He stood up from the table and tossed the picture to the floor as he made his exit.

"I'll be in touch with that information!" Zya called after him, speaking to his back as he walked hastily out of the room. Zya knew of Ethic's ability to hustle but she had no idea of his track record in gunplay. She had just flipped a switch that had turned on the beast in him and after today, nothing about him would ever be the same.

Chapter 8

Rage burned in Ethic as he pulled his hood over his head. It was a rainy night on the Brooklyn block and nothing was moving. Nothing except a dead man walking. Zya had made good on her promise and sent the address to his phone shortly after their meeting. He had been tailing Mizan for hours. Part of him wanted to see that Mizan had turned his life around . . . he hoped that maybe seven years had been enough time for Mizan to find remorse. Ethic knew that once he committed this murder then there was no claiming to be out of the game. He was jumping back in head first, which was why he wished that God would intervene and show him a man that had changed, redeemed himself after his monstrous acts. Maybe then Ethic wouldn't . . . *Nah, cut the bullshit though . . . for real, for real.* It didn't matter if Mizan was feeding starving babies in Africa when Ethic ran up on him; he was going to leave the nigga leaking. Someone had to pay for the loss of his child's mother. There had to be some sort of consequence that made up for the reprieve of justice. He knew that he should just let it go. A vengeful soul had a way of becoming a damned one, but there was no way he could let Mizan keep breathing after what he had done. He had come so close to killing him. In fact Ethic had broken so many bones in Mizan's body the day that he had run up on him that he was within an inch of his life. The only thing that had spared Mizan was the fact that he was hot. He had been under investigation when he had walked into Ethic's trap and the cops raided the spot before Ethic could finish the job. They both had been arrested that day and Ethic had spent a year in prison for aggravated assault. By the time he touched down on the streets Mizan was long gone and Ethic's desire to finish the job had gone unfulfilled until now.

Ethic picked up the pace of his step as he came up on Mizan's left. His hand palmed the .357 snub that he concealed in his hoodie. Just as they were passing an alley that sat between two closed storefronts Ethic pushed Mizan between the buildings.

"Hey, bro! What the fuck! I ain't got shit, homeboy!" Mizan exclaimed as Ethic used his forearm to pin Mizan against the brick wall.

"Remember me?" Ethic asked as he removed the hood as he gritted his teeth while cutting off Mizan's air flow. He jammed the gun deep into Mizan's rib cage and his face twisted as recognition flickered in his eyes. His eyes widened in fear. They say your life flashes before your eyes in the face of death, but Mizan's life had been one of fuck-ups. There was nothing for him to reminisce on. Tears came to his eyes and Ethic scoffed. He had always known that Mizan was made up of pure bitch. There was nothing gangster about him. "You know what this is for," Ethic sneered through clenched teeth. He looked Mizan in the eyes. The seconds felt like hours as Ethic made a mental note of the fear that he saw in Mizan. He had waited for this moment for a long time and without further hesitation he pulled the trigger.

Psst!

Psst!

Psst!

He couldn't stop his finger from curling on the trigger until his entire clip was empty. The silenced bullets ripped Mizan's insides to shreds and Ethic let him go as his body weight crashed to the ground. He didn't even stay to watch as Mizan drowned in his own blood. It would only take a minute or two for Mizan to die but it would be the slowest and most painful sixty seconds of his life. "Bitch-ass nigga," Ethic mumbled as he wiped off the dirty gun and tossed it down the alley. He lifted the hood once more and then disappeared into the night; with a heavy heart but a lighter conscience he made his retreat.

YaYa powered on her phone and it immediately came alive in her hands. Indie had left her ten voice messages, even Miesha, and Elaine had attempted to reach her several times. She refused to answer. She just wasn't ready to talk to anyone. What did they want her to say? What could they possibly say? Nothing would make the pain go away. Indie's past had come out to bite her in the ass and instead of making love to her husband on their wedding night she was drowning her sorrows in a bottle of Merlot. She desperately wanted to call and hear Skylar's voice because she knew that it would be like a bandage to her soul, but nine times out of ten Skylar was with Indie and she wasn't ready to hear anything he had to say. She turned off her phone and tossed it on the couch as she leaned her head back on the cushions. Tears slid down the sides of her face and she swiped them away stubbornly. The sobs had stopped hours ago, but for some reason she couldn't stop fresh pools of emotion from seeping out of her eyes. The tears were continuous and no matter how hard she willed them away they fell like trickling raindrops. Her chest had never felt heavier. She was lovesick but in the worst way. It felt like she was suffocating, choking, gagging on her own grief.

Knock! Knock!

The unexpected sound at the door caused her heart to skip a beat. *How did he find me?* she thought as she immediately assumed that Indie had somehow found her. *I wouldn't be surprised . . . this nigga has people on payroll everywhere!* she thought, exasperated. She was ready to ignore him but the sudden urge to slap fire from him caused her to rush to the door. She pulled it open as she yelled, "I don't want to see you!" She was surprised to find Ethic standing before her. The hurt in his eyes radiated between their gaze and in that moment she knew that he was the only person who could relate to her pain. She didn't know what was weighing on him but she knew that it was heavy. "Ethic? What are you doing here?" she asked. She could smell the cognac on him as he stood before her, eyes heavy with sadness and a stress that she hadn't noticed earlier.

"I don't know," he said in a low tone of devastation. Earlier when she had met him he seemed so strong. He had the smooth confidence that only a real man could possess but this man who had shown up at her doorstep looked lost. It was like in a matter of hours something so drastic had occurred that it had sucked the life out of him. She knew that it wasn't impossible, however. Life seemed to change as quickly as the blink of an eye and once pain settled into your bones it was hard to shake.

"Come in," YaYa offered as she stepped to the side.

"I'm sorry, ma, it's late. I shouldn't have come here," he said as he shook his head trying to shake the ominous feeling of sorrow that he felt.

"Come on," she said as she grabbed his hand. "You look like you could use a . . ." She paused when she noticed dark specks all over his hoodie. She had been in the game long enough to recognize blood as soon as she saw it. "Ethic, what happened tonight?"

Ethic looked at her and she could tell that he was mentally debating whether she was trustworthy. Honestly the deadly look in his eyes made her not even want to know, but this man, this broken, beautiful, man who had helped her, now needed her help . . . even if all she had to offer was an ear to listen.

"If I tell you something that I'm not supposed to tell anyone, will that make you trust me enough to tell me what's on your mind?" she asked. The wine had her loose at the lips and the devastation that she felt over her interrupted nuptials caused her to look for companionship in Ethic. She was grateful that he had come back because she was afraid to be alone. When it was just her and four walls she was forced to think about Indie, about the bitch Parker, and the so-called baby they shared. Nope, Ethic's distraction was much needed.

"I don't think your secret matches mine, gorgeous," Ethic said with a slight smile.

The way that he spoke to her wasn't obnoxious. He had a way of delivering a compliment that was so genuine she couldn't do anything but accept it. He wasn't gaming her, but simply speaking his truth. He was giving it to her the way that he saw it and he didn't filter himself for anyone. She appreciated his honesty.

"You think I'm beautiful?" she asked.

"I think you know you're beautiful. I think it's something you've heard your entire life," Ethic replied. "I just think whatever happened today is making you doubt that."

A silence fell over the room and Ethic immediately regretted bringing up her wedding. He clasped his hands and said, "Okay, you share your secret and I'll share mine."

"I think you killed someone today," YaYa said. Ethic immediately tensed as he stood to his feet.

"This isn't a good idea. I was out of line coming here."
He started for the door but YaYa stopped him.

She grabbed at his hoodie and continued, "You don't
have to tell me if you did or not. I just think that's what
happened. I can tell because you have the same look on
your face that I had when I caught a body. There's blood
on your shirt," she whispered. She unzipped the hoodie
and helped him remove it as she stared in his eyes. "Are
you okay?"

Ethic closed his eyes and she stepped closer to him as
she intertwined her hands with his.

"Ethic . . ."

He pressed his forehead against hers but he couldn't
look her in the eyes.

"I promised myself that I wouldn't be this person
again. That I would never show my kids this side of me.
That this kingpin shit . . . the game . . . the hustle . . . the
life would never affect them. I slipped up tonight," Ethic
said.

"It's okay," YaYa whispered. "Look at me."

Ethic opened his eyes and the vision of her concerned
face mesmerized him. Her green eyes were hypnotizing
and in that moment of weakness he felt her strength.
They knew nothing of one another but what they felt was
undeniable. They understood each other. "I murdered
the nigga who murdered my son's mother. I've waited a
long time to put that play down and it didn't fill the void
like I thought it would," he admitted.

"Hate doesn't fill the void where love used to be," she
said. "It doesn't fit. I understand the need for revenge.
For years I played that game but it will eat away at you
if you allow it to. You killed him, he's gone. He paid for
what he did. Now you just have to let go."

Her voice soothed his weary soul and he placed a hand
on the side of her face. She leaned into him instinctively

as she gave him a genuine smile. "You're going to make an amazing wife. He's lucky," Ethic whispered.

She sadly looked down at her bare ring finger and replied, "This finger wouldn't be empty right now if he felt that way. If a complete stranger can see it, why can't he?" *Damn, here go these fucking tears again,* she thought as the burn of betrayal stung her eyes. She inhaled and blew out a sharp breath as she shook the feelings that were threatening to crumble her. She didn't know this man standing in front of her and he clearly was dealing with his own demons tonight. She couldn't let him witness her breakdown. "There's blood spatter all on your clothes. You can use the bathroom to shower," she offered. "I don't think you should drive tonight and I already had a plan to get fucking faded," she said with a chuckle. Laughing was the only thing she could do to keep from crying. "You're halfway there already. I could use a drinking partner to get me that way. So stay. I don't think either of us should be alone with our thoughts tonight."

"You always have sleepovers with dangerous men?" Ethic asked, curiously, as he wondered why he didn't intimidate her.

She smirked as she thought of her days of tricking hustlers out of their paper. Even Indie was no saint. In fact, she had a thing for danger. She had lived life on the edge for so long that even when she wasn't trying, she attracted a certain breed of men. She saw nothing but gangster in Ethic and the type of experience that came with years in the game. He was a boss and she knew it . . . he knew she knew it, too.

"I've had one or two in my lifetime," she replied, smiling. "But none of them seem quite like you. You're the king of an empire somewhere. The difference is you don't seem to want to be." She turned and said, "You can use the spare bath. There are towels inside. An extra robe is hanging in there as well. If you bag your clothes I can call the concierge to have it dry cleaned by the morning."

"Thank you," he said sincerely.

"Thank you for coming back," she said. "I don't know what made you come here when you could have gone anywhere else, but that knock at the door saved me from a long night of feeling sorry for myself."

Ethic emerged from the shower with a towel wrapped around his waist, still wet as beads of water dripped down his sculpted chest and abs. YaYa was frozen as she admired him. He was a beautiful specimen of a man but the fact that he wasn't overly arrogant as he stood before her made her smile.

"You think those abs and arms, and chest, and God that face is going to seduce me?" she asked playfully. "This is something straight out of a romance novel." She laughed. "That game is played."

He chuckled heartily at her wit and the sparkle in her eye. "I'm glad this amuses you. There was no robe," he said.

"Follow me, there is one in the master bath," she replied. On the way she grabbed the glasses of wine that she had poured and handed him one.

"Wine isn't going to nurse those emotional wounds, ma," he said jokingly. "We're looking to forget our problems for the night, not heighten them. We need something heavier."

She sipped her glass as she handed him the plush hotel robe. She turned around so that he could slip out of the towel. When she turned back around she smiled. "You look like you feel better," she said.

"Good company does that to you," he answered. He walked up to her and removed the glass from her hand then grabbed her wrist as he led her out to the bar. He had purchased the penthouse suite, which came with its own fully stocked center. "Have a seat, beautiful. I'm going to be your bartender for the night. Now if you want to forget about your disaster of a wedding . . ."

She cut her eyes at him and pointed her finger. "Hey, no jokes. It's too soon!"

He laughed and she admired the handsome features of his face. Ethic wasn't perfect. In fact, the scars on his face had left one side slightly ugly. She recognized them as burns because she too had similar marks from the house fire that she and Leah had been trapped in. What should have been considered a flaw, however, she found completely endearing.

He poured her a shot of Patrón.

"Tequila?" she asked doubtfully.

"I thought you were a big girl," he challenged.

She rolled her eyes and then took the shot, grimacing as it burned on the way down. He immediately poured her another. She hit that off too.

He followed suit and then leaned over the bar, letting his elbows rest atop it. They stared at one another silently. What should have been an awkward beat was really an appreciated connection that they shared. YaYa hadn't felt this comfortable with anyone in a very long time. Even Indie hadn't penetrated her soul in this way lately. Although she loved him, she sometimes felt as if the things that they had been through together had left a sour aftertaste in their relationship. They had hurt one another so many times that their love while still true, had been diluted some. Ethic didn't know her past, therefore he couldn't judge. She had never hurt him; therefore he didn't hate any piece of her. Most importantly he had never betrayed her, so she held not even the slightest resentment toward him. All she felt for him was affection . . . new, uncomplicated affection. She was slowly determining that he was a good man with a fucked-up past and that was the exact story of her life.

She reached out to touch his face and he tensed slightly. "I'm sorry," she whispered. "I'm not trying to be rude. Can I ask what happened?"

He exhaled, releasing the tension from his chest. "That's a long story," he said.

She rounded the bar and stood in front of him. "We have all night. I want to know who you are," she said.

Ethic poured himself a real drink this time, pulling a bottle of Louis off the shelf and dropping a few ice cubes in a glass.

"I used to supply an old friend of mine and his daughter Raven fell in love with a bad guy. She was young, he was older and he saw her as a come-up. The nigga manipulated Raven to get close to her father's empire. My friend was murdered and eventually Raven was murdered too. A bomb was placed under a vehicle I was riding in. It should have killed me, but it didn't. Some people say I was lucky, but I was left many scars . . . The ones you can see aren't even the worst. It's the shit that plays over in my head that hurt the most," he admitted. He had given her the short version of the story but it was still the most that he had ever shared with anyone. "The nigga I murked tonight was responsible for Raven's murder."

"I'm sorry," YaYa said as she frowned in concern.

"It's okay, it was a long time ago, ma," Ethic said.

"Then why do I still see the love you have for her in your eyes?"she asked.

He chuckled as he shook his head. "You didn't know Raven. She wasn't the type of woman that you forget," he whispered nostalgically. She could tell that he was lost in his thoughts and a part of her was jealous. What had happened to her and Indie? Why didn't she see that look of love in his eyes when he looked at her? It had been there in the beginning but somewhere along the way it had disappeared and she hadn't even noticed.

"You're an amazing man, every part of you, even the gangster part that you're ashamed to show," she said.

"I haven't met anyone that was this easy to talk to in a very long time," Ethic replied.

"I was just thinking the same thing about you," she said honestly.

The two stayed up for hours, laughing as their conversation lasted until dawn. YaYa didn't even realize that she had fallen asleep until she woke up, nestled inside his tight grip. At first she panicked, thinking that something had happened between them, but when she realized that she was fully clothed she exhaled in relief. She closed her eyes, enjoying the feeling of his strong arms around her as her back pressed into his chest. She hadn't felt this secure ever. Even with Indie there was always some kind of fear in her heart, but in this moment she felt completely sheltered. She knew that time was fleeting, however. In real life, her world was in chaos. The temporary bubble that she had dwelled in the night before was about to be popped. Ethic stirred behind her and she turned around to face him.

"Good morning," she greeted.

"Good morning," he replied. A knock at the door caused her to rise as she went to answer it. "It's the concierge with your clothes!" she announced. She grabbed the clothes and rushed back into the room.

"I guess that's my exit cue," he said as he stood to his feet.

"Unfortunately so," she replied. "I'll give you a moment to dress." As she went into the living room an anxious pit formed in her stomach. It was like a great date was coming to a close. She desperately wanted to see Ethic again. They just clicked. It was like they were kindred spirits and a part of her was sad that it was time to say good-bye. He emerged from the room and she smiled. "Good as new. I have to thank you again . . . for rescuing me yesterday."

Ethic nodded his head and looked at her as if he wanted to say something but instead he held his tongue. "Good-bye, YaYa," he said. She felt a pain in her chest as if cupid had tried to pull an arrow from her heart. It sounded so final and she was filled with disappointment because she knew that it was. They were strangers and once he walked out of the door she would never hear from him again.

"It feels like I know you. Like I shouldn't be letting you just walk out the door," she admitted.

"You have a life to get back to, a man that is wondering where you are. If I could take you away from it all I would, but your home is here. Your heart is here, it's just in pieces right now," he said. He walked up on her and planted a kiss on her forehead. She closed her eyes and savored the moment of intimacy. "I hope everything works out for you, ma."

"Good-bye, Ethic," she whispered. As soon as he walked out of the door she let her body fall to the couch. She laid her head back on the cushions and reached for her phone. It was time for her to check back in with reality, whether she wanted to or not. If she didn't there was a new bitch in town by the name of Parker who was just waiting to take her place.

Chapter 9

Indie's thoughts raced as he sat in the driveway to his parents' home. It was the first time that he had ever felt as if he didn't belong. He was all over the place. He had no idea where YaYa was and Parker's revelation had put him in a precarious position. He couldn't help but ask himself the inevitable question. If Parker hadn't been run out of town, would he have been preparing to marry her instead of Disaya? To know that his mother had orchestrated the entire thing only made it that much worse. He hadn't even been able to face her. While he had been blowing up YaYa's phone, Elaine had been calling his nonstop. Her persistence was an admission of her guilt. Disappointment, anger, resentment . . . He wasn't used to aiming those emotions at the woman who had birthed him but he couldn't contain them, not when something so big had been at stake. "I have a son," he whispered. That fact would surely change his life forever and he couldn't help but wonder how Parker's presence would impact YaYa. *She's going to leave me,* he thought in despair. Indie was truly stuck between a rock and a hard place. Not only was Parker telling him that they shared a child, she was asking him to come back to her. She wanted him and once upon a time she had been all he wanted. It was only the greatness of YaYa's presence that made him forget about Parker. Before that, Indie had been miserable without her. Now that Parker was back, whom would he choose? His past or his future?

Indie opened the car door and used his key to enter the beautiful home. He had built it for his parents from the ground up. It had been a token of his appreciation for them . . . a symbol of love. When he was getting money he always thought that his parents were the only people in the world he could trust, especially his mother, but now he questioned that. The woman who he thought would never lie to him had omitted the most important truth. It was time for her to lay her cards on the table. The smell of food filled the air and he followed his nose to the kitchen. Elaine stood making a huge Southern breakfast, a Sunday tradition in her household. Skylar sat at her feet, coloring in a children's book happily. His father sat, completely distracted by the *New York Times* that he was eyeing intently. He and his new wife were supposed to be sitting at the table, enjoying their first official family breakfast before departing for their honeymoon. He couldn't believe how quickly life had gone south.

He stood back silently, leaning against the wall as he watched his mother move around the kitchen like an expert chef. He had so much respect for her, so much love. Before yesterday he never would have imagined that she would betray him.

"Good morning," he said, making his presence known. The sound of his voice caused Elaine to freeze but she kept her back turned to him.

His father glanced up from his paper. "How's it going, son?" he asked.

"Not so good, Pops," Indie replied.

Elaine cleared her throat. "Bill, could you take Skylar in the other room? Indie and I have some things to talk about," she said.

Bill had never been the one to intervene in their mother-and-son disagreements and he wasn't going to start now. He stood to his feet and scooped up his grandchild, but before exiting the room he stopped in front of Indie. "Take it easy on her. She may meddle and she may cross the line sometimes, but she loves you and she would do anything to make sure that you are okay."

Indie nodded and kissed Skylar's forehead; then Bill walked out of the room.

Elaine turned finally to face him as she dried her hands on the kitchen towel. "I guess Parker told you," she said.

"How could you, Ma?" he asked.

"You weren't ready to be a father. You had your entire life ahead of you. You were headed to college. A baby would have thrown you off track," Elaine reasoned.

"I was only headed to college because of Parker. Before her I was full blown in the streets. You know that. I don't have to remind you. I was running with Nanzi and his crew until I met P. It was her that made me apply to school. I only had my head in the books because that was the kind of guy she liked. She was going away to school and if I didn't too, I was going to lose her. She was a good girl, why would you run her off? We could have been—"

"You couldn't have been anything, Indie!" Elaine said. "She was pregnant at seventeen. I wasn't about to let her destroy your entire future. I paid that girl to get an abortion. Gave her good money to leave town and never look back. It might not have been right, but it was a decision that I made for my child. I had no way of knowing that she never went through with her end of things. You think I would allow any grandchild of mine to be out in the world and not know me?"

"I don't know what I think about you anymore," Indie said. "And just so you know, Ma, Parker not being around was the reason I dropped out of college. I wanted to be that type of man because it was her type. Without her there with me, it was all for nothing. It was because of your meddling that I went back to the streets and here I am ten years later and I'm still in them. You know what she did, Ma?"

Elaine's silence caused him to proceed.

"She's a college professor," he said. "Imagine what I could have been if I had stayed with her. She was a good girl. She didn't deserve what you did to her."

"What you became isn't enough for you? I did what I thought was best," Elaine said, holding firm, despite the conflict that was tearing her apart on the inside.

Indie pushed his finger down on the table as he spoke his next words with emphasis. "You were wrong." He stood up abruptly and walked out of the kitchen before he cut into her with disrespect. He had tried his hardest to stop his sharp words from cutting her. He had never felt the fire he had burning inside of his chest—not toward his mother; she was usually the one to calm him—but the things that she had done had altered the fabric of his life drastically. She had ultimately set him up in a three-way triangle with YaYa and Parker. Both of them deserved his love, both of them he loved dearly, and one of them was going to end up hurt all because of Elaine. He grabbed Skylar and her belongings.

"Everything okay?" his father asked as he walked Indie to the door.

"Help me out here, old man," Indie said. "What do I do?"

"You do what's right," Bill replied.

Indie nodded his head as he guided Skylar out the door. His head was so clouded that he couldn't decipher right from wrong. Whose interest should he have had at heart? YaYa's? Parker's? Maybe his own?

No matter whom he chose or what he did, none of it seemed right. In fact, nothing had ever felt so wrong.

***

"Mommy!" Skylar yelled as she rushed into Disaya's arms as soon as they walked through the door.

The sound of her daughter's voice was like music to her ears and she bent down to pick her up. She lifted the little girl over her head and smothered her with kisses. "Mommy missed you, Sky!" she said jovially. Her daughter's tiny arms squeezed her so tight that they immediately made her feel loved. She never even looked at Indie, although she felt him standing there, staring at her. He didn't deserve her attention.

"YaYa, can we talk?" he asked.

"Nope," she said, ornery as she walked right passed him with Sky still in her arms. "You want to watch a movie with Mommy, baby?"

"Yay! Movie time!" Skylar shouted happily. Indie knew this routine. Whenever YaYa only spoke to their daughter she was pissed beyond measure. Her blatant disregard for his presence was understandable and he exercised patience as he followed her up to their bedroom.

"YaYa?" he repeated.

She sighed as she turned to him. He could see the myriad of emotions just from the look that sorrowed her face. Her sadness couldn't be hidden, no matter what kind of front she put on. She was trying to mask her misery with anger, but he had always had the ability to stare into her soul. He could feel the ache that replaced the beat of her heart. He could feel the lump that lodged in her throat. He shared her pain, but she doubted him all the same. She didn't know whose team he was on. Hers or Parkers? YaYa knew that this wasn't a conversation that she could avoid and she placed her child on her feet. "Go to your room, baby," she instructed. They both waited until Skylar was out of earshot before they spoke. "What can you possibly have to say to me, Indie? You embarrassed me! A bitch stormed in during our wedding claiming to have your child and you told me to give you a minute?"

"I didn't know what to do," he admitted.

"You didn't know what to do?" she scoffed in disbelief. "You should have kicked the bitch out. Instead you left me hanging, standing there in front of hundreds of guests while your dirty laundry played out for every-fuck-ing-body to see!" She was shouting, she was so angry but Indie kept a cool head because he knew that it was justified. She was entitled to feel this way. To argue with her would only infuriate her more.

"Where did this girl even come from? I've been with you for years, holding you down, loving you, giving you every piece of me. Has she been in the background all this time?" YaYa asked, coming unraveled as the thought of Indie being unfaithful ran rampant in her mind.

Overwhelmed with grief she couldn't stop herself from bawling as she sat down on the edge of the bed. Seeing her so torn, so broken, ate away at Indie. He had put this hurt on her heart. No matter how unintentional this all was, it still unnerved him that she was burdened so heavily.

"No, ma. I've never cheated on you," he said. "You're my everything, YaYa. I need you to believe that."

She shook her head as she looked up at him, tears drenching her face, eyes red. Worry lines creased her forehead. "I don't know what to believe. All I know is that this hurts. She has your son?"

"She says she does," Indie admitted.

"And you believe her?" YaYa asked.

Indie hesitated before answering. There was no breaking this news lightly. He knew how serious he and Parker used to be, but he decided to spare the details. Telling YaYa that Parker was his first love would only make things worse. "I'm not sure," he lied. "If the kid is mine—"

"I know," she interrupted. "You don't have to tell me that. You'll be there. The question is will you still be here?" she asked. Before he could respond she got up and walked away, dismal and completely lost because she no longer knew what her future held.

Chapter 10

Parker's skin felt like silk as the bubbles from the steaming bath she was submerged in covered her body. The scent of vanilla filled the air and she sunk even deeper as the warmth slowly melted the tension away. Moving back to New York had seemed like the right thing to do. For years she had missed home, missed Indie, but now that she was here so many complications stood in her way. She had never expected Indie to have so many attachments. Even if he decided to give up his current life to reunite with her, she knew that it would not be a simple transition. He came with baggage now. Another child and that child's mother . . . There was guaranteed to be drama. Parker loved Indie, but she wasn't beat for the bullshit. Even thinking about it caused a mini-headache to commence. She cursed herself for not coming back earlier. Had she found the courage to admit the truth years ago, perhaps Indie would have never found a new love. She remembered how intense their love affair used to be. After she had become his girl there was never a time that you would see Indie without seeing her. They became quick friends and faster lovers. It was a whirlwind courtship and she held on to the memories like they were a valuable keepsake, tucking them away in her mental under lock and key. She remembered it all as if it was only yesterday. . . .

Click-Clack!

The sound of a shotgun being cocked caused Parker to jump out of her sleep. She was immediately greeted by the barrel of a gun. "You scream and I pull this trigger. You got me?"

Two men in ski masks stood before her. "Please . . ."

"Shut up and lead me to the safe," one of the men ordered.

Fear paralyzed Parker as she stared death in the face. "You do what you're told and I won't pop your melon," he said.

"In the office," the other one spoke.

Her eyes shot to the clock above their heads. It was 2:00 a.m. Big Jim was still tucked away in one of the rooms recovering from his romp in the sheets with one of the local working girls. Little did the burglars know, he was the only one who could open the safe. They had no wins with Parker. She backpedaled slowly as the two hooded figures eased her into the office and drew the blinds.

"Please don't kill me. I'm seventeen. I'm a senior at—"

"Didn't I tell you to shut the fuck up?" masked man number one shouted as he hit her with the barrel of the gun. The force of the blow was so powerful that it sent her flying to the ground in distress.

"Agh!" she cried as she grabbed her face. As she pulled her shaky hand away from her brow she saw blood flowing between her fingers. She felt it as it trickled down the side of her face.

"Yo, bro, chill the fuck out!" the second man spoke up for the first time as he grabbed the violent thug by the arm, forcefully. "You know the deal. We here for the money. In and out." Her internal alarm sounded off as soon as she heard his voice. I know him, she thought in disbelief. Oh my God. That's that guy . . . Indie.

She immediately turned her attention to him. "Please I just work here, I don't have access to anything other than the front desk money and most guests pay with a card."

"Yo, this bitch is lying," the unknown masked man spit aggressively as he yanked her from the floor. "Where's the fucking safe?"

Indie stood watch at the door while his brother, Nanzi, handled the heist inside of the office.

Parker shook as terror seized her. Her mind drew a blank. Being slapped out of her sleep by a robbery had paralyzed her. She couldn't form a sentence to cooperate if she wanted to. She knew the deal. She had come up around stick up kids her entire life. Once they got what they wanted from her they were going to kill her. She didn't want to die but she knew that her breaths were fleeting. Every second that past were the last moments of her life. They say that your entire life flashes before your eyes but as she looked down the barrel of her gun, she didn't see her past. All Parker could see was the times she hadn't lived yet. She saw her future, everything that she had not had the chance to do. The places she hadn't seen.

"Please don't kill me," she pleaded.

Whop!

Parker's jaw felt like it cracked in half as the man brought his gun across her face full force. She saw nothing but white as pain blinded her. It was so tremendous that it felt like a thunderstorm had erupted in her brain.

"Yo, man! Fuck are you doing? I said don't hurt her. We here for the money. Stay focused," the lookout stated as he stepped inside the office and pulled her attacker off of her. Recognition flashed in Parker's eyes as a face flashed in her mind. She knew that voice.

Oh my God. It's the kid Indie.

She immediately grasped at his arm, clinging to him for dear life. "Please, please don't hurt me." With the two intruders inside the office there was no one on watch to see Big Jim easing into the office with his shotgun aimed.

Click-Clack!

"You motherfuckers tryin'a rob me?" Big Jim shouted as he pulled the trigger. Big Jim put a buckshot in the shoulder of Indie's accomplice.

On instinct Indie turned and put a bullet between the fat white man's eyes.

"Aghh!" Parker screamed as she watched his body drop to his knees before falling face first into the ground. Blood poured out of him and pooled around his body as it began to leak in her direction. Indie turned the gun in her direction but when he saw the fear in her eyes he lowered it. Instead of firing, he rushed to his brother's side and helped him off of the floor. Blood leaked everywhere as Nanzi screamed in agony.

Sirens rang out in the distance. "Let's get the fuck out of here," Indie stated.

"Fuck that safe, bro, let's go!" Indie stated as he tried to pull his brother toward the door.

"Nigga, we didn't just catch a body for nothing," Nanzi shouted. He grabbed Indie's gun from his hand and aimed it at Parker. "Bitch, open that fucking safe before I blow your top the fuck off."

Parker scrambled to the desk and pulled out the drawer, frantically. She didn't know the combination but Big Jim was as predictable as the weather. Her hands shook so badly that she could barely turn the dial to the correct numbers. She tried his birthday to no avail.

"Bitch, don't play with me!"

She felt the steel on the back of her head. "Agh . . . I'm not! I'm not!" she hollered while sobbing as she tried his home address.

"Man, come on!" Indie screamed.

"Indie, please!" she screamed, desperately.

"This bitch knows your voice?" Nanzi shouted.

Finally Parker opened the safe and as Nanzi's finger wrapped around the trigger Indie snatched the gun. "Get the shit out the safe and let's go."

"Man, don't be stupid! This bitch knows you by name!"

"I won't say anything. Please I swear!" Parker promised as tears and snot made an emotional disaster on her face.

"You heard her. Let's dip," Indie decided.

Nanzi nabbed the contents of the safe and shook his head as he spat. "You're lucky."

The two raced out of the hotel and hopped into the awaiting car before speeding into the night.

Parker curled up into a ball as she buried her head into her knees, crying hysterically. By the time the police burst on to the scene Indie was long gone, but the ramifications of the robbery had left Parker in mental pieces.

Parker's world moved in slow motion as she answered the detective's questions. The dead bodies were still on the floor at her feet and she was in a state of shock as she tried to recall the night's events. The police grilled with repetition trying to see if she was in on the take, but her answers were always the same. She knew the street code; despite the fact that she didn't believe in it, she still followed suit. By the time they were done with their interrogations they were more frustrated than the high school witness. When they allowed her to leave she didn't look back. With her hands stuffed in her pockets she kept her head low as she headed home. She just wanted to put as much distance between herself and the hotel as possible. The sound of the gunshots kept ringing out in her head. She was terrified. The chill in her bones had nothing to do with the winter cold; it came from the *horrific double murder she had just witnessed. She was so distracted by her thoughts that she never saw Indie pull alongside her.*

He tapped his horn twice and when she saw his face she took off running down the block.

"Fuck!" he shouted as he sped up after her, cutting her off at the next cross street. He threw the car in park and then hopped out. They were only a few blocks from the crime scene and the last thing he needed was to draw unnecessary attention to himself. "Get in the car, I'm not going to hurt you," he reasoned. She backpedaled as he approached her.

"I didn't say shit to them, I didn't. I swear to God. Please just let me go home," Parker pleaded frantically, a mixture of fear and confusion dancing in her wide eyes. Indie held out his hands to show her he meant no harm. He had never seen a person fear him the way that she did. He felt a tug of guilt pull at his heart as he realized that what he and his brother did had traumatized her.

"Whoa, whoa, ma, I'm not going to hurt you. I just want to talk to you," he said. She turned to run but Indie quickly grabbed her arm. "Listen to me. If I was going to hurt you I would have done it already, right? I'm not going to hurt you. Trust me. I promise."

She stopped struggling when she saw the look in his eyes. She believed him when he said that he wouldn't hurt her, but that still didn't make her compliant. She snatched her arm away and said, "Stay away from me!" She rushed away from Indie, her feet moving in a slight jog as she tucked her head and stuffed her hands in her pocket. She just wanted as much distance between them as possible.

Going home was like walking into a brothel. It wasn't that she looked down on her mother or sisters. It was just that she wanted so much more. She wanted to be

*seen for more than her ass and her thighs or the curves
of her hips. While her sisters had taken every lesson
from their mother to heart, Parker knew that to view her
body as an asset was the same as selling her soul. Assets
could be bought and sold, they had a monetary value.
Parker knew the power of her blooming womanhood at
an early age. It wasn't the "P" that made great men kneel
at the feet of greater women; it was the minds of those
great women. She knew that beauty without brains was
pointless but because she was the youngest of her clan,
her voice was inaudible, her reasoning ignored. The
smell of Mary Jane was strong as she made her way
to her room. This place was almost worse than a hotel.
More men ran in and out of this spot than they did the
professional establishment. She knew that she wouldn't
be there long. It wasn't enough room here for her. It was
a house full of grown women who rarely worked; too
many periods and not enough peace. Parker wasn't beat
for the bullshit. She was the youngest one in the bunch
but despite this she was the wisest.*

*"What the hell happened to you?" her sister Tisa asked
as Parker walked into the room that they shared. Tisa
stood applying makeup to her already pretty face. That
was one thing about the Banks sisters. They were all
equally gorgeous. They came in all shapes, all sizes, all
complexions, but the genes that constructed them were
the same. They shared the same button nose, the same
chestnut eyes, and mess of curly ringlets they called
hair. Their hips, their breasts, their lips, were all cut
from the same cloth physically, but mentally they were
miles away. Parker just couldn't get with the mindset
of "closed legs don't get fed." That was for brainless
females. Parker wanted to be so much more.*

*She was visibly shaken as she peeled herself out of her
bloodstained clothes.*

"Nothing," she whispered.

Tisa stopped what she was doing and turned toward Parker. "Parker?"

Parker shook her head and got on her knees as she grabbed her personal items from under her bed. Living there she had to hide all of her stuff so that no one else used them. It was survival of the fittest. She didn't even keep her bath towel in the bathroom for fear that one of the strange men that ran in and out would use it. Cum stains were as common as the roaches on the walls in her home, which was why she often slept in one of the vacant rooms at the hotel.

"I said nothing happened," Parker snapped.

She wrapped herself in her housecoat and headed to the bathroom. She could hear the sex sounds oozing out of the rooms of her other sisters. Even her mother entertained a different man every night. None of them worked, so they got their money on their backs. They were selling themselves short and exposing Parker, the youngest member of their family, to all kinds of chaos in the process. She went into the bathroom and sighed in relief as she turned on the shower. The small unventilated space quickly fogged as she stepped into the tub basin. She couldn't believe what had happened that night. Sounds of the gunshots still rang in her ears and as she let the water rinse the dried blood from her body, she cried. Even when she tried to do the right thing, the wrong things always found a way to wreck havoc on her life.

The creak of the door opening caused her to freeze. "Tisa, is that you?" she asked. When she got no response she turned off the water and pulled back the shower curtain. She almost jumped out of her skin when she found, Gutter, her mom's sometime boyfriend, standing there, gawking at her naked body.

"What the fuck are you doing? Get out!" she screamed.

He advanced on her, stepping into the shower and pressing her against the tiled wall as he groped her breasts.

"Stop! Ma!" Parker screamed as she tried to push him off of her. His 220-pound frame was too much to fight off, however, and he put his fingers in between her legs, penetrating what had never been penetrated before.

"No," Parker sobbed.

He brought her wetness up to his lips and said, "I'm going to get into this tight little pussy whether you want me too or not, you stuck-up little bitch."

He pulled away just as her mother and sisters burst through the door.

"What the hell is going on in here?" her mother shouted, while holding a joint in her hand. Her robe was open revealing the cheap lingerie beneath.

"Ain't nothing happening, baby. I'm just trying to take a piss," Gutter lied.

"He attacked me!" Parker shouted, distraught.

"Girl, ain't nobody tried to attack you," her mother defended.

"He put his hands on me! He touched my—"

"Shut up Parker!" Her mother said.

"I'm out of here. A nigga don't need this bullshit," Gutter stated.

Her mother's face twisted in angst as she turned to Parker. "See what you did!" She chased after him. "Gutter. Baby, don't leave. She can leave. She don't pay no bills here."

Tisa and her other sisters shook their heads and dispersed, unfazed by the drama. They each had been through it with one of their mother's boyfriends. They were so immune to the concept of saying no that they now allowed anyone to touch them anywhere.

Parker stormed out of the bathroom, tears flowing, temper raging as she quickly slipped into her clothes. She grabbed anything of importance that she could carry. After tonight, she wouldn't be coming back. This hellhole was worse than anything the real world had to offer. She didn't care if she had to sleep on subways at night and attend school in the day; she refused to ever close her eyes under her mother's roof. If the price of rent was pussy, she'd pass. She flung her book bag over her shoulder.

"Where are you going?" Tisa asked.

"Anywhere but here," Parker shot back. She stormed right passed her mother coddling Gutter's grimy-ass and out the door. As soon as she stepped outside her building, however, Indie was there, waiting for her, perched on the hood of his car.

She stopped dead in her tracks. Fear was real that night. If she left she was in danger. If she stayed she was in danger.

"Yo, shorty, I'm not here to do nothing to you," Indie said as he held his hands up.

She was shaking and crying. Her wet hair curled into a mess on top of her head.

"Please don't. Please, just let me go. I need to get out of here," she whispered.

Indie frowned because her panic wasn't just about the robbery. The way she kept looking behind her made him think she was running from something.

"Who you looking for? What you running from?" Indie asked.

She didn't know why she told him, but she responded, "My mother's boyfriend, Gutter."

"Gutter?" Indie asked with a frown. "That nasty-ass old nigga?" Gutter was a known low-level hustler around the way that had a reputation for being a creep. Many young

girls had accused him of rape and Indie immediately saw red. "He touch you?" Indie asked.

She nodded and he raced up the stairs, pulling her along with him. "Show me where the nigga at?"

She pulled against him. "Please I can't go back in there."

"Gutter!" Indie roared, causing several residents in the apartment building to peek out of the doors.

Gutter emerged from the apartment at the end of the hall. "Fuck is you, li'l nigga?" he asked.

Indie didn't hesitate. He pulled his pistol off his waist-line and put it straight to Gutter's forehead.

"Whoa, li'l daddy," Gutter said immediately bitching up. "Whoa, whoa."

Indie pressed the gun hard against his flesh. "You see that girl right there?" Indie asked pointing to Parker.

Gutter flinched beneath Indie's wrath, fearing the inevitable bullet that would end his life. "I don't know what that bitch told you, playboy," Gutter began.

Indie slapped him with the butt of his gun. Parker's sisters and mother peeked out of the apartment, but didn't say a word.

"You fucking lay one finger on her again and I'm going to fucking kill you," Indie stated. He was so mad that he spit as he spoke. "You got me?"

Gutter nodded. "I got you," he said as he urinated on himself from fear.

Indie looked down at the pool of liquid that stained Gutter's pants and he shook his head. "Old ass, perverted mu'fucka." He stepped back and aimed at Gutter's hand.

Boom!

He blew all five fingers off without hesitation. "That's for putting your hands on her, you bitch-ass nigga. Next time I'm putting two in your chest."

He turned around and led Parker out of the building. "Let's go, shorty. You're safe with me," he promised. Parker's mouth hung open, astonished, but she didn't say anything. She simply took his hand and followed him out to his car. He tucked her safely inside and then entered the driver's seat before skirting off into the night.

Her intuition told her she could trust him but she had no idea that he would be the guy that she would fall in love with. Only fate knew that Indie and Parker's love story was written in the stars.

"Shorty, open the door."

Parker emerged from the water, bringing her head above the warmth as she swept a hand over her face to clear her eyes. Being submerged had drowned out the sound of her surroundings, but . . .

I could have sworn I heard his voice, she thought as she looked around the bathroom. *What the hell? Am I hearing things?* she thought as she breathed a sigh of relief. Her imagination had run so wild. Daydreaming of what used to be had made her feel euphoric, so much so that she was imagining things. She hadn't heard Indie call her by that nickname since she was a young kid. So much had changed since then. Most for the better, but she had been through the worst in order to get this place of self-sufficiency without him.

Knock! Knock!

A soft tap at the door alarmed her to the point where she drew in a sharp breath.

"Hello?" she called out.

"Open the door, ma, it's me."

Parker gasped as she hopped out of the warm bath and immediately wrapped herself in a towel. "One second!" she said. *What the hell is he doing here? How did he even get in my room?*

She rushed to the vanity mirror and tried to fluff out her wet curls, but her natural state wasn't to be tamed lightly, especially in the blink of an eye and at the motivation of Indie Perkins. She pulled her hair up in haste, subduing it in a messy, kinky bun. "Fuck it," she whispered. She quickly dressed in jeans and a tight fitting V-neck T-shirt then opened the bathroom door. She marched out into the living room area of her suite.

"Most people call first," she said as she walked passed Indie and headed directly to the mini-bar. She grabbed a bottle of water out of it and leaned against the wall as she gave him her full attention. "What did you pay the maid to let you in here?"

"My apologies, P, you can withdraw your claws. I came here to talk," Indie said. "Things haven't been too peaceful at home. I couldn't think clearly so I thought you could help me sort all of this out."

"I don't know if I can do that for you, Indie," she said. "I've laid my heart out on the table. You have a situation already. The ball is in your court. You have to choose."

"It's not that easy," Indie said.

"I know," she admitted. "And I'm sorry. I'm not blind to the fact that I've complicated things for you."

"That's putting it lightly," he shot back with the smile that she loved so much. She had forgotten just how beautiful of a man that he was. As he stood before her in all his glory, casually clad in jeans and Timbs, he reminded her so much of the kid she had fallen for years before. So much about him had changed. His status, his bank account, his boyish charm . . . but her infatuation with him had remained. She hated this uncertainty that was in the air. There was an invisible wall of tension, of betrayal, of mistrust, of fear . . . they both felt it and it took up all the space like an elephant in the room.

"I really missed you, Indie. So much," she said, honestly. She spoke so lowly that he almost couldn't hear her. As she stared at him she pinched her arms as they crossed over her chest. She needed to feel the hint of pain to tell herself this wasn't a dream. He was here in front of her. "You don't know how many times I've cried at night because you weren't next to me." The ache in her voice was real as she turned away from Indie to stop herself from becoming emotional.

The sight of her alone tugged at Indie's heart strings. The first love was always the toughest to shake. Indie had no worries about YaYa's loyalty because he was her first love. Every nigga before him had been looked at as a come-up. Indie on the other hand had an entire love affair with the woman standing before him. She had been out of sight out of mind for so long that he had forgotten how strong of a hold she had been over him. Once upon a time, Parker was all that he had lived for. Seeing her hurting was like a magnet. He felt his feet moving toward her. He knew that he should keep his distance. To get to close to her would be setting himself up to fall in love all over again. He couldn't betray YaYa that way. Despite what she thought at the moment, he loved her, but he would be lying to himself if he didn't admit that he loved Parker too. Could it be possible? To love two women at the same time yet for different reasons?

YaYa, his Disaya . . . since walking into his life she had turned it upside down. She was elusive and defiant, but her weaknesses were what endured him to her. He wanted to protect her, be there for her . . . show her how to love and be loved. Her smile was like a masterpiece painted by the hand of Van Gogh and each day with her was exciting. Each day held a different high or low. There was no middle ground with YaYa, no ordinary, no average. She was either everything or nothing at all. It was love or war between them but Indie appreciated every moment with her. Being with her felt like living because both joy and pain reminded him that he was alive.

But Parker . . . Parker Banks was like a summer breeze on scorching day. Everything about her was refreshing. Parker's beauty was so simple that it was magnificent. In a world full of fake she was as authentic as it came. From her heart to her hair to her soul she was one hundred. Their connection was more than physical. It was mental and those waters ran deep. She was the type of beautiful that was everlasting and after years in the game, encountering her again at this point in his life was like a breath of fresh air. Her depth and perspective was something that he would never find in another woman. She had been this way since they were teenagers and from day one she had captured his heart. He allowed her to hold it in the palm of her hands because he was certain that she wouldn't break it. With Parker he could be vulnerable. He could let her lead him into legitimacy because no part of her had ever been anything else. She was a good girl, nah . . . that's inaccurate. She was a great woman. She embodied everything that it meant to be a woman.

Indie wished that he could combine them to make the perfect woman but he wasn't naïve. He knew that in a world of imperfections, perfection was only a wish.

"What do you want from me, P?" he asked. "What do you want me to do, ma? There is no right or wrong. No matter what decision I make, I'm losing."

She turned to him. "I'd like you to meet your son," she whispered. "I know that all you can think of is the life you would be giving up if you chose me, but I need you to see the possibilities that exist my way."

The thought of a son warmed him and he pulled her closely. He grabbed the back of her neck and she laid her head on his chest. "I'm going to figure this out. I promise you that, Parker. I want to meet my son though. I want that more than I've ever wanted anything. Me and you . . . me and YaYa . . . I don't know how any of that will work out, but I do know that no more time will go by without me being in his life."

She pulled away from him and gave him a weak smile. "King is curious. He wants to know you. He needs to know you."

"You named him King?" Indie said, shocked.

"It's what we always said we would name our first son," she whispered. "And he was made from one so it was only suiting."

As Indie looked Parker in her eyes their souls melted. The feeling was so familiar because he had been there before. He knew exactly what it felt like to love this woman and he couldn't deny the fact that the feelings were ever present. He leaned in, unable to contain what he was feeling. He went to kiss her lips. Parker caught his face in between her hands as she halted him.

"There is no back and forth with me, Indie. When you kiss me I want to know that I'm the only one you're kissing. I want to be your only, not your option, not some side chick. I don't do that. Any woman with any kind of self-love would never do that. I'm not that girl."

Indie kissed her cheek instead and before he pulled away he whispered in her ear. "That is why I love you, P. You're a queen and you remind me that I have to be a king in order to keep you. I'm going to fix this."

"You pinky swear?" she asked, bringing their old thing back. It was the one thing that they never broke. To pinky swear was like putting it on the Bible . . . the sacredness of their relationship. She held out her pinky and he locked his with hers.

"I pinky swear, ma," he answered.

He headed out and before he opened the door she said, "You can meet him, tomorrow. We can take the train to DC and you can meet your son." She paused for a beat. "If you want to."

"I'll be here," he replied.

Indie walked out of the hotel distracted by the gifts and curses that his wedding day had produced, but before he could process any of it his cell phone came alive in his hand.

> We need to talk . . . in person. 9 p.m. You know where.
> –Z

The message from Zya was enough to put his mind back on the money. It was a welcomed distraction from the game of tug of war that was going on inside his heart.

Chapter 11

Business. Hustle. Money. It was all a welcome distraction from the circus that had become his life. As he rode in the back of the tinted black truck he wondered what the motivation was for Zya's summons. They were now legit. With Indie as a shareholder in Vartex Enterprises, their transition into pharmaceuticals would prove to be beyond lucrative. All they were waiting for was the FDA approvals to come through. Indie had access to prescription drugs and with Zya as a silent force behind him, he intended to establish a network that spanned from East to West. Some would never understand his new disinterest in cocaine, but what niggas didn't understand was that pills were where the real money was. Pills didn't discriminate. Niggas, bitches, black, white, young, and old had all found the new vice as a means to fly and he was singlehandedly going to subdue the game. All he had to figure out was distribution. He hadn't forgotten about his new role in the company, he had simply put it on the back burner. He needed every move to be made with clarity and at the moment he was all over the place. Indie didn't want to squander his new position amongst the powerful and legit at Vartex, by making rash decisions. His next move would be his best. As his driver pulled up to the private airstrip, he grabbed his Louie duffel out of the seat next to him. He pulled a crisp one hundred dollar bill out of his pocket and handed it to the driver.

"Thanks, boss. Let me get the door for you," the forty-something driver said. Indie could recognize a street nigga when he saw one. The jail tattoos on the man's hands told a street story of years past that the man had obviously lived. Indie respected the fact that the man was now in business for himself. Despite the fact that Indie was moving on a much grander scale, he could relate to the driver. He didn't want to be the oldest hustler hugging the block. That was worse than the old bitch in the club. He wanted to sever his ties with the coke game and make his money real. Street money could only go so far. He needed bank records, tax returns . . . He needed something that the Feds wouldn't kick in his door to take. Security. That's what he was searching for and he respected any man who had been able to obtain that for himself, no matter how meager the endeavor.

"Nah, I got it. Thanks for the ride," Indie said as he popped the door open and placed one foot on the ground.

"Hey yo, boss, here's my card. I don't know what kind of business you're into and all, but if you ever need a car service again, I'm your man." He passed Indie a business card. Indie accepted it and gave him a nod as he extended his hand.

They shook as Indie read the card: "Louise Vincent," he said. "Will do."

The single stewardess waited at the bottom of the steps as Indie approached.

"Good evening, Mr. Perkins. The pilot is ready to lift the wheels. Welcome," the brunette greeted with a friendly smile. He nodded and ascended the steps. Making the trip to Italy was unexpected but when Zya summoned, he knew it was important. No matter what was going on around him her call was one that he would always have to take. YaYa had understood this without fuss because she had once been in his shoes. She was wise to the ins and outs of the game. She knew exactly what it took to be in his position so when it was time to move he received no protest from her direction. She was his ride or die, but in that moment he couldn't help but wonder if Parker would be as understanding. They were worlds apart. Parker's degrees didn't mean shit in his world and her lack of knowledge regarding his dealings would keep her bitching in his ear. *Why are you even entertaining what P would do? That's not your concern. She's not your girl,* he scolded himself as he finally entered the cabin. He couldn't help but feel some type of accountability to his woman and since his disastrous wedding day, Parker and YaYa had been included in his thoughts.

He moved to take a seat and was completely thrown when he saw another passenger sitting on the plane. He halted his step and squared his shoulders as he instinctively put his hand near his waistline. Gangster recognized gangster and Indie could automatically sense that he was in the presence of a rare breed. He knew because he was bred the same. He looked back to the stewardess with a look of confusion.

"He is a guest of Ms. Miller's as well. The two of you will be making the trip over together. Please let me know if you need anything," she said.

Indie locked eyes with the man who nodded his head in acknowledgment.

Indie nodded and then took a seat directly across from the surprise passenger. He didn't want to sit behind the man because he didn't want to pose a threat. He had no idea who the man was, but he knew that if he was a guest of Zya's it was a bridge that she was about to connect him to. He needed to keep things copasetic until he could figure out who and why he was here, but he for damn sure wasn't sitting up front. Many men had suffered the fate of death by being too trusting. He would never allow anyone to put a gun to the back of his head and pull the trigger. So he was smart. He sat on the other side of the aisle all the while wondering, *Who the fuck is this nigga?*

The ten-hour flight was filled with tension as both men kept to themselves. Neither closed their eyes to rest on the way across the pond. Built the same, Ethic and Indie were two men who recognized a real street nigga. Being in each other's presence was like the clash of the titans. Their egos were on high and their awareness on full alert. Ethic glanced over at Indie. As soon as he had stepped foot on the plane he had noticed the bulge on his waistline where he holstered his pistol. He wouldn't rest easy until that gun was locked up in the cockpit. He didn't know Indie. He barely knew Zya and he had no idea what he was getting himself into. They were on some international kingpin shit and that level of hustling was new to Ethic. He was a made man in his own right, in his own territory. The Midwest had been his for the taking, but when Zya informed him that he'd be taking a trip to Italy to finalize their deal and meet her business partner he knew that this was an entirely new gig. He was a pertinent piece to her distribution puzzle and he was stepping into the major leagues. The Sosas. The Escobars. Zya moved at their level and Ethic was being offered a seat at her table. The test of silent will he was having with Indie wasn't his style so he decided to extend an olive branch. They had long travels ahead of them and Ethic was tired as hell. He wasn't about to sleep with one eye open.

"My man, I'm Ethic," he said as he leaned over and extended his hand.

There was a brief pause before his gesture was returned. "Indie," he greeted.

"I don't know about you, but I'm not trying to be on guard for the rest of the flight," Ethic said as he removed his gun. He ejected the clip and took the bullet out of the chamber before placing the shell on the seat next to him. "I don't know you. You don't know me. You keep the gun until we land. Without the clip it's useless. You get my drift? Maybe I can get some rest if I'm not worried about a new nigga popping my melon on the way over."

Indie was hesitant and Ethic continued, "You've been yawning and shit for the past hour. This way both of us can get some sleep."

Indie smirked and then emptied his clip and popped one out of the head. The men exchanged weapons.

"I was tired than a mu'fucka, man," Indie admitted with a slight chuckle.

Ethic laughed and finally relaxed as he lay back in the plushness of the private jet as they made the trip overseas to see the one woman who had brought them together.

"Good to see you, gentlemen, I'm glad your travels were safe," Zya said as she stood at the bottom of her opulent staircase while watching them walk into her Italian villa.

Her property was exquisite and she looked like royalty. She was the queen of this castle and she was ready to connect with these two to expand her empire. She was a kingpin, fuck a queen. She played second in command to no one, but even being the best in the game was not enough for Zya. She wanted that corporate money.

"Welcome, Ethic, it's good to see you again," she said as he leaned down to kiss her cheek politely.

Indie followed suit but when she greeted him she paused for a moment. "Are you okay?" she asked in a low tone so that only the two of them could hear.

He nodded in confirmation.

"Is she?" she pushed.

"She will be," he assured.

A look of sympathy crossed her face as she offered, "If you need anything . . ."

"We're good," he confirmed sternly, letting Zya know that his personal relationship wasn't up for discussion.

She noticed his standoffish demeanor and she replied, "Good. Then its time to get back to business." She walked off. "Follow me, gentlemen. My chef prepared a spread for you. You must be starving after a ten-hour flight."

Zya spared no expense when it came to catering to Indie and Ethic. As they sat down on the vast lawn of her estate, overlooking the small Italian town that sat below the hills, they sipped champagne and ate the finest Italian dishes. She got down to business. "So let me explain to you why you're here," she said. "Ethic runs a trucking company out of Flint, MI. In the past seven years he's built his company up to a multimillion dollar business. Given that he used to move more weight in the Midwest than both of us combined, it doesn't surprise me that he was able to build his business so quickly. The best part is he had government contracts with several cities, which means that his company is reputable. His drivers get stopped less frequently and they aren't under the scrutiny of local cops. This makes him the perfect person to transport our goods."

"And what exactly are your goods?" Ethic asked. "I'll need to know exactly what I'm moving. Weed? Coke? Pills?"

"We are moving away from street drugs. Indie is a shareholder in Vartex," Zya informed.

"The pharmaceutical company?" Ethic asked, intrigued.

Indie nodded and responded, "I got my foot in the door recently and now it's time to plant the money trees."

"The rate has already been discussed," Zya informed Indie. "Ethic and I have struck a deal that will get us all rich. The purpose of today is to introduce the two of you. Is this something that we all are still interested in doing? Many operations have been toppled by trying to force chemistry among partners. If it doesn't fit, it doesn't fit."

"Business isn't personal. As long as you hold up your end of things I give no protests," Indie said, directing his words toward Ethic.

"Good," Zya said as a smile spread across her beautiful face. She knew this was the beginning of something epic. "I have a network of doctors who want to buy their meds on the black market. The drug companies' prices are too high. They want to come through us. We'll also put Oxy, Xanax, Adderall . . . We'll run those through the streets."

"Do you trust your drivers?" Indie asked.

"I have a few in mind for these runs," Ethic answered. "They don't need to know what's being transported. The less they know the more normal they'll behave. The pills need to be concealed in other packages. Something discreet."

"I can work that out," Indie assured.

Zya couldn't help but smirk. Her boys were playing nice and the good vibes meant good business. She raised her glass and cleared her throat before proposing a toast. "Here's to power," she said.

The threesome tapped champagne flutes and as they indulged in their meal and drinks Zya stood to her feet. "Enjoy your time here in Italy, boys." She turned to Indie and finished, "I'll leave it up to you to make sure he is a familiar face to your shooters. Acclimate them to Ethic so that there will be no unnecessary tensions. When the two of you get back to the States it'll be time to put in work."

As she made her way back up to the house while two beautiful models made their way toward Indie and Ethic.

"See to it that they are well entertained, ladies," she instructed as she slipped them a hefty payment.

She left Indie and Ethic to their playthings as she made her departure.

Chapter 12

YaYa was grateful for Indie's impromptu trip out of town. It was the only time that she didn't worry about his whereabouts. As long as he was tied up in business with Zya, he couldn't be with Parker. They had never had that type of relationship. Never had she been so insecure about her place in his life. Suddenly this bitch had come to town and rocked her entire world. YaYa's heart burned with jealousy and resentment. She didn't care that Parker had come way before her or that the Indie shared a child with her. It didn't seem fair that this storm had come into their lives without warning. Confrontation was on her brain like cancer, plaguing her, illing her to the point where her stomach was in constant knots. In the blink of an eye she had gone from queen pin, to Leah's victim, and now to concerned wifey. She had never thought she would play that role . . . the bitch who lost sleep because her man's loyalty was uncertain. *This can't be life,* she thought as she rifled through Indie's things. Here she was checking pockets and drawers. She was disappointed in herself, but it didn't stop her from opening a full-blown investigation on her man. This entire situation was Indie's fault. He should have put Parker out on her ass the moment she disrupted their nuptials, but when he didn't YaYa's antennas went up. She knew her man like the back of her hand and she saw the hesitation in his eyes when he looked at Parker. There was something between them and not time or distance had put out that

flame. YaYa wasn't going to leave her life up to chance
and she wasn't about that competition life. The day Indie
made her go head up for his love would be the day he lost
hers for good. She looked around the room at the mess
she had made and couldn't help but wonder how things
had come to this. "Get a hold of yourself," she whispered.
She bent down to pick up the disarray when she noticed
a napkin hanging out of the pocket of Indie's jean pocket.
She picked it up and opened it. The London. It was the
logo printed on it and she dropped it instantly as if it was
hot to the touch. YaYa saw red as she made up her own
interpretation of why Indie had visited the hotel. It didn't
matter how she tried to cut the situation, all roads led
back to Parker.

He was at her hotel, she thought. Her throat went dry
as tears came to her eyes. She didn't even think of the fact
that she herself had spent the night with a man she barely
knew. Nothing had gone down between them, despite the
fact that Ethic had crossed her mind a time or two since.
Indie didn't get the benefit of the doubt. His interaction
with Parker was more than a chance meeting. They had
history and YaYa could sense it in every fiber of her body
that Parker was a threat.

Fire pulsed through her veins. Heated beyond measure
YaYa stormed out of her bedroom in search of her daughter. "Sky! Baby, where are you?" she called out, bravado
shaking her voice as she willed herself not to cry. A million
scenarios played through her head. *Did he fuck her? Why
was he at her room? Is he going to leave me for her?* Just
days ago YaYa's feet were firmly planted on the ground and
in the blink of an eye everything had changed. Now she
seemed to be freefalling through life. She had finally found
the semblance of peace after Leah had died, but Parker had
appeared out of nowhere. She was the new bitch in YaYa's
life, but this was one battle that she didn't intend on losing.

Leah had gotten inside of her head; she had weakened her. YaYa wouldn't give Parker the chance to. She was going to be on the offensive instead of waiting to defend. Fuck it. If Parker had the balls to burst into her wedding ceremony unannounced than YaYa certainly had the balls to pay this bitch an unexpected visit. A part of her wanted to leave Skylar with Elaine. She didn't want to take her child along just in case anything popped off, but she feared that Elaine would try to stop her. So against her better judgment she decided that Skylar was coming. She had to be sure to act accordingly now that her mini me was coming along for the ride. She found her daughter sitting on her bedroom floor, playing so peacefully. She was the most precious thing in YaYa's life. Everything about this beautiful brown baby was beautiful and the perfect mixture of YaYa and Indie. So many times she had been the glue in their relationship. Skylar deserved a father and a mother that defied the odds and stayed together. Her heart melted and now more than ever YaYa wanted to fight for her family. The beautiful angel who relied on her was worth the fight no matter how hard it may be. She told herself that she would not confront Parker with aggression. She wanted to talk. That was all. YaYa deserved to face off with the woman who had ruined her wedding and more importantly Parker needed to hear that YaYa wasn't lying down to take an L. She would fight tooth and nail for Indie because there was so much more at stake than just her winning a man. He was her friend, her confidant, her soul mate, her everything. Indie was the only other person in the world who knew what it felt like to parent her daughter. He was the only other person in the world who could read her thoughts. They had been down together and he had loved her in moments when she was completely unlovable. Through tricking and drug use, even when her heart was painted black with revenge, Indie had loved her. Men weren't made like him nowadays. No one wanted the tough love. No man was willing to stick out the bad days. They wanted bad bitches. Perfect wifeys to sport as arm candy yet wouldn't put up a fuss. YaYa had been none of those things. She was so far from perfect that she was in the realm of wrong but he still stayed. He still loved her. No, YaYa wasn't giving that up. As she rubbed her daughter's head lovingly she whispered, "I love you, little girl. I'm so sorry for all of the things I have done wrong as your mom. I'm going to get it wrong a lot of times, but I can promise you that I will always try. Nobody is going to destroy our family. Nobody."

She knew that Skylar didn't fully understand what she was saying. In fact, Skylar hadn't even looked up from her toys, but YaYa meant every word. She grabbed her hand and said, "Come on, baby, follow me." She wrapped Skylar up and slipped shoes on her little feet and with a heavy heart she made the trip into Manhattan.

YaYa stood in front of the hotel room door as adrenaline pulsed through her body. Had this been five years ago, YaYa would have come beefing, ready to slap fire from Parker's ass for the stunt that she had pulled. There was still a part of her that wanted to hold on to that young girl from the hood, but she knew that she would only be putting the ball in Parker's court. The lump in her throat made it hard for her to swallow as she stood, listening to her heart as it beat loudly in her ears.

"Mommy, where are we?" Skylar asked in a toddler's babble.

"Mommy is just visiting a friend, Sky. I need you to be a good girl," she said as she held on to her daughter's hand.

"Okay, Mommy," Skylar replied.

YaYa took in a sharp breath and held it for a beat before releasing it slowly as she knocked on the door. She didn't know what to expect, but she was prepared for anything.

When the door finally opened YaYa was prepared to state her case. She was prepared to give Parker a few choice words for the fiasco she had turned the wedding into, but she was completely taken off-guard when she saw the little person at the door. Her eyes drifted downward to the boy before her and her heart immediately sank into her stomach. Tears burned in her eyes as she stared into the face of this child. Nothing had ever hurt so badly. There was no doubt about it. This kid belonged to Indie. YaYa knew it because he looked exactly like Skylar. They shared the same eyes . . . the same lips . . . the same complexion. This was Indie's son. It felt as if the air had been sucked out of her lungs as she stared into this boy's eyes and her hand trembled as she grasped her own child's hand.

"King, who is it at the door?" Parker's voice called out from inside the suite. When she appeared at the door YaYa immediately noticed the shock in her face. She stepped in front of her son as if she had to protect him and YaYa held on to Skylar a bit tighter. The faceoff. Woman to woman. Lioness against lioness, both fighting for the king of the game and protecting their cub. That's what this was. They were both after the same thing and the tension was so thick that both women forgot to breathe. They were stuck in the moment, neither realizing how draining this moment would be when they were finally face to face. YaYa surveyed Parker and immediately felt disgust. She was pretty but plain and after what she had pulled YaYa was almost sure that on the inside she was horrific. YaYa hated her in that moment. She became so many "bitches" in YaYa's mind. The only thing that stopped YaYa from popping off and telling her exactly how she felt was the children who were standing in their presence.

"What are you doing here?" Parker asked.

"You don't have the right to ask me that question after the episode you pulled on my wedding day," YaYa said.

YaYa picked Skylar up and pushed past Parker as she entered the suite.

"What are you doing?" Parker said.

"I'm making myself comfortable. Sit down. You and I are going to get a few things straight," YaYa demanded.

Parker hesitated but YaYa persisted. "I'm not leaving, so you may as well sit and start talking. We can do this the civil way or I can drop my daughter off and come back to do it the way I want to. Things can get real very quickly. You don't know me but I can tell you that you definitely don't want that," YaYa said.

Parker sighed as she turned to her son. "King, please take . . ." She looked at Skylar, realizing that she didn't know her name.

"Skylar. Her name is Skylar," YaYa said.

"Why don't you and Skylar go into the bedroom and turn on cartoons, baby," she said.

"Okay, Ma," he said. He walked over to YaYa and extended his hand to Skylar. YaYa's heart fluttered because he reminded her so much of Indie. A mixture of love and resentment swelled in her chest.

"Can I go, Mommy?" Skylar asked.

"Yeah, Sky, you can go, baby," YaYa replied.

"I'll take care of her," King said and YaYa smiled slightly because she believed him. She watched the kids disappear into the bedroom. They had no clue that they were even related, let alone siblings.

"Well this is awkward," Parker quipped as she folded her arms across her chest as she took a seat in the chair across from the sofa where YaYa was seated.

"What do you want?" YaYa asked.

Parker sighed. There was no simple answer to that question. She wanted it all. The man, the house, the family, the future children. When Parker looked at Skylar she saw a seed of the man that she loved that had been planted somewhere else. What she wanted was too complicated to explain. She wanted to rewind time and go back to before she ever left NYC. She wanted to fix the broken heart that she had left Indie with. She certainly didn't want to tear apart another woman's family but if that's what she had to do in order to reclaim her spot in Indie's life then yes, she would.

"I want what has always belonged to me. I want a father for my child. I want Indie," Parker whispered truthfully.

"That won't happen," YaYa replied. "You have the audacity to come into our lives talking about some bullshit high school fantasy that you had of y'all living happily ever after. You ruined our wedding day! You make a spectacle of our union. I have every resource at my disposal to make your ass a memory, but I'm trying to see your side of this. I'm trying to be the bigger person here, but this 'I want Indie' shit is testing me."

Parker scoffed and replied, "You should feel threatened. What Indie and I have is incomparable. I would hate me too if I was you."

YaYa tightened her jaw and she responded through gritted teeth. "Hate you? Sweetheart, you're cute. You really are. You're irrelevant. You can stroll down memory lane all you want but in the end Indie is going to still be with me. If you thought I was going to just let him go, you're mistaken. I'm not the type of enemy you want to make. The last bitch who thought she could beat me took her last breaths in front of me." YaYa reached into her purse and pulled out a large manila envelope filled with cash.

"This is $150,000. It's all I had lying around the house. When the banks open Monday morning I'll withdraw $350,000 more. It's yours. Tax free, but there is one stipulation."

Parker interjected, "Let me guess, stay away from Indie?"

"Forget you ever knew Indie and leave New York," YaYa said.

Parker felt the flicker of fear in her heart as she stared YaYa in the eyes. She had definitely underestimated the amount of fight YaYa had. "What is this? A gangster movie?" Parker asked. "You can keep your money because me and my son aren't going anywhere. I don't take too kindly to threats either. In your world women probably jump at the opportunity to make that kind of money. They will do anything for it. Fuck, suck, probably even kill. I'm sure you've done a lot more for a lot less, but a real woman can't be bought. A real woman has self-respect, but you wouldn't know anything about that," Parker said slyly. "I don't need a hook-up because I know how to come up all on my own through hard work. My son deserves a father and after Indie meets him there is no way he is going to turn his back on us. So get real used to seeing me. YaYa is it? Because me and that little boy in there are going to be around whether you like it or not. Now take your dirty money and get out."

YaYa grabbed the money off of the table. "Suit yourself," she said. She stood to her feet and adjusted her clothing slowly. "You're wasting your time. That plain Jane, independent woman, good girl act might have worked eight years ago, but Indie don't want that now. He got a thing for bad bitches that you'll never understand and from what I'm looking at you're not even equipped to compete. Your entire vibe is just too"—she paused for a beat and then scoffed—"boring. Indie being responsible for his son . . . I have no problem with that. It's you who doesn't fit. My man has never been and will never be accountable to another woman. He sleeps next to me every night and he will continue to do so. You can hang on with your side chick tendencies for as long as you want, but you will never have him. He will never be yours. Every holiday, every birthday, every reason to celebrate will be done with his family . . . every accomplishment shared with me . . . and it will be me to ease his tensions after a hard day of work. It will always be me. Skylar and I. You will never be apart of that. King, maybe, but you never. You better tread lightly because if I wake up on the wrong side of the bed one day I might send somebody over here to get that ass, just for payback for the stunt you pulled at my wedding. Indie is my man, my soon-to-be husband. Whatever the two of you had is dead. You respect that and we won't have problems. You disrespect that and you're going to find your son calling me Mommy, while you're on the outside looking in. I'll cut you so far out of Indie's life that you will regret ever coming back. Don't believe me? Try me," she said.

As if on cue Skylar came running out of the bedroom and grabbed YaYa's leg.

"Come on, baby, Mommy's done here," YaYa said.

"Bye, Skylar," King said as he came running out of the room as well.

The toddler waved and YaYa smiled as she held her hand out to the child. "Good-bye, King. It was very nice to meet you," she said. She turned on her Loubs and stormed past Parker, knowing that this was the first battle of many to come.

Chapter 13

Parker pinched the bridge of her nose as she exhaled sharply. YaYa had come through her suite like a hurricane, disrupting her peace and now her mind was wrapped up in a mental storm. She had wanted to say so many things, but instead she held her tongue because she knew that in the end she was wrong for interrupting another woman's wedding the way that she had. She had known that she would be making a new enemy when she came back to town. YaYa had good reason to hate her. No sane woman would have done what Parker had, but love was on the line and when dealing with matters of the heart it was always insane.

"What's wrong, Ma?" King asked.

"Nothing, baby boy," Parker responded. "I'm fine. I need to talk to you."

She kneeled so that she was speaking to him at eye level and she rubbed the sides of his arms lovingly. *Maybe I shouldn't have come back here,* Parker thought. *We were doing just fine without Indie.* Parker wanted to believe that she had the independent woman role down but she was simply using it as a mask to hide the emptiness she felt. She needed a man, but not just any man would do. She had dismissed so many guys, some of them excellent candidates for a husband and father, all because she had never let go of her first love. Indie was it for her, but now she wondered if she had come back to NYC for the wrong reasons. She had told herself that she was coming because

King needed a father and a part of that was true, but she also needed Indie. She never thought of the family she was destroying in the pursuit of restoring her own. Maybe it was best if she stayed in DC. The type of beef that YaYa was bringing to her doorstep was more than she had been prepared to handle. YaYa had practically threatened her life.

"King, I know you want to meet your father but—"

Before Parker could even finish her sentence her son interjected, "But what? You promised, Ma. All of my friends have their dads at the games. I just want mine there too." He tried to keep his voice steady but Parker heard the tremble in his tone.

She looked at him with sympathy. His hurt was her hurt and it was great. A boy needed his father. If she had given birth to a girl she may have been able to pull off raising a child alone. She knew how to teach a girl how to become a young woman. She knew how to guide a girl into adolescence. Had King been a queen, this would have been much easier for her to do without help, but she was raising a boy. She had the fate of a young black man in the palm of her hands. She didn't know the first thing about being a man. She knew nothing of a black man's struggles, of his strengths, of his inner fears. A boy needed a man to look up to. King needed Indie. She truly believed that a lack of fatherhood was the reason why so many black boys became black slaves to the prison system. She would do everything in her power to reunite her family. *Fuck YaYa and her family,* she thought harshly. As she looked in her son's eyes she blinked away her tears and gave him a reassuring smile. "Don't worry, baby. I'm going to make sure you meet him. I promise."

The Day Parker Fell in Love with Indie Perkins
Knock! Knock! Knock!
3:00 a.m.

The red numbers that flashed on her digital alarm clock reminded her that she only had three more hours until she had to wake up for school. These late-night visits always threw her off, but like clockwork she rose out of her bed and walked to the front door. She placed her fingers on the security chain and said, "Is that you?"

"Open up," he replied.

She released the chain and flipped the lock then twisted the knob to welcome Indie into her home. Well technically it was his home. The apartment he rented for her was in his name. He only came by to drop off his money and check on her to make sure things were all right.

"Why don't you just use the key?" she asked groggily as she wiped her eyes and locked the door once he was inside.

"This is your house, ma. I got it for you. Just because I can get a key doesn't mean I deserve one. I want this to be your space. Your rules. You had enough of niggas running in and out of your mama's crib without your permission. You don't have to worry about that here, even with me," he said sincerely. "I want you to trust me."

"I do trust you," she replied honestly. "Where's the package?" she asked.

Indie reached in waistband and pulled out two thick bands bills of various faces. He tossed them her way and she caught them out of midair.

"What's this? Twenty?" she asked. She could practically look at a stack of money and tell how much it was. That's how accustomed she had come to handling it. Indie kept his safe at her house. He had her ducked off so that he didn't have to fear anyone running up in the spot. Parker disappeared into the bedroom and popped open Indie's safe. For some reason that she didn't even under-

stand, he trusted her with his combination. Rightfully so, because she had never lifted a dollar of the $80,000 that he had saved so far. She was like his accountant and kept track of every dollar.

At first glance Parker had thought Indie was your average dope boy. He was attractive and flashy with an ego that was on ten. Indie symbolized everything that turned Parker off, but for some reason she couldn't help but find herself falling for him. The fact that he had seen a need and fulfilled it for her without hesitation had endeared him to her. Once they had actually begun to get to know one another she immediately recognized the intellectual within. Indie was highly intelligent and had the charisma of a man twice his age. He came from nothing but wanted everything, which was why he stayed in the streets with his older brother Nanzi. He was just chasing the American dream, or at least his version of it. She counted out $22,000 and added it to the contents in the safe, before securing it and returning to the living room.

"What's the count?" Indie asked.

"102," she replied.

"You bring your books?" Parker asked.

Indie's head fell back as he sighed. "It's three a.m., shorty, can't we do this tomorrow?" he asked.

"No, we can't. You have a test tomorrow," she said. "That was the deal. I'd let you keep your product here if you went to school every day and let me help you study. You want to graduate don't you?"

"You want me to graduate," Indie mumbled. Parker cocked her head to the side and looked at him incredulously. She went over to the front door and held it open as she propped a hand on her hip.

"Well since we're not going to study I guess you don't need to stay the night," she said with her brows raised in a challenge.

Indie conceded as he nodded his head. "A'ight, ma, crack open the books."

At first Indie had aligned himself next to Parker to guarantee her silence. She was the only person who could ID him as the second shooter in the motel robbery and he needed to insure his freedom. What had started as an ulterior motive had quickly developed into a powerful friendship and a growing attraction that he couldn't ignore. Parker was different from all of the other girls their age. The chicks around the way hopped on his dick without second thought. He had run through more than a few simply because he was gaining a heavy reputation in the game. They were impressed by things . . . cars, clothes, jewelry and they had nothing inside of their small heads. Indie could literally have his pick of the litter and he wanted none of them, at least not for anything more than a night. Parker, however, she possessed a depth that kept him on his toes and intrigued the hell out of him. She was smart and she believed in him so much that Indie believed that he was smart too. He had always known that he was slick, but smart? He spent most of his time in the streets and only went to school enough to keep his mother off his back. Since meeting Parker and seeing how focused she was on her studies made him respect her. He had a hustle plan to get rich before he was twenty-five, but she had one of her own. She was dead set on a college scholarship and for some reason she made him think that there was more than one way to make it out of the hood. Indie was completely infatuated with her. He was digging her, which was more than he could say about any other girl. No one else had ever been able to hold his attention this long and he hadn't even hit yet. The last thing he was trying to do was leave her presence. After a long night on the block, around her was exactly where he wanted to be. He made his way to the small kitchenette that he had purchased for her.

"You just gon' stand there or we gon' get started, Einstein?" Indie asked jokingly with a small smirk.

She relaxed and closed her door before walking back over to Indie. She pulled a chair next to him and opened the books that were already sitting on the table. She opened them up and said, *"We've got a test tomorrow that I'm sure you haven't even attempted to study for. So it looks like we will be pulling an all-nighter."*

Hours passed as they quizzed one another, laughing and getting to know one another as they conversed. This was a nightly ritual for them. He'd hustle and show up on her doorstep at unspeakable hours. Most niggas associated a drive-by after midnight as a booty call, but Indie knew that she would stimulate so much more than his loins. He passed his mother's house every night and drove an extra thirty minutes just to see Parker. He needed the mental stimulation she provided and on top of that her smile . . . it was the most radiant he had ever seen. As they closed their books after a long night, Parker asked, *"Why don't you apply yourself more?"*

"School ain't for everybody, P," Indie replied.

"That's true, but it is for you. You're stupid smart, Indie. I've checked your transcript—"

"You what?" Indie asked, defensively. He wasn't a report card type of kid. He hadn't opened his since sophomore year, when his older brother had introduced him to ounces.

"Don't get mad. You know I have service for my last hour so I pulled your file. Your grades are decent. You're not a dummy. If you actually tried, you could graduate with a decent GPA. You could go to college. You're smart, Indie. You don't have to hide your money in safes and sell drugs to your own people. You can be so much more," she said whimsically as if she had dreamt of his future before.

"What I am isn't enough?" he asked.

Parker nodded her head and said, "Yeah, it probably is . . . for the girls in short skirts and six-inch heels."

"But not enough for you?" Indie asked.

His question threw her off-guard as her mouth fell open but no words came out. She and Indie weren't in the same league. He was the cool kid. The dope boy. He was the one that all the girls wanted. *Guys like you aren't attracted to girls like me,* she thought.

"Indie . . ." Her head fell as she looked down, unsure of how to respond. A guy like Indie could derail all of her plans for greatness. He was handsome and distracting and . . . He lowered his head as well until their foreheads met.

"You want to make me a bet?" he asked.

"Huh?" she responded, confused.

"If I get an A on this bullshit-ass test we been losing sleep over, you have to let me take you out," Indie said.

"What? Indie, where is this coming from?" she asked.

"You make me see things differently, P. I never thought I'd care about grades or college or none of that bullshit but because it's important to you, it's become important to me. You have become important to me," he said.

She paused as she thought of what he was saying. He had no reason to game her . . . or to lie. "I'm not your type," she replied.

"And that's what I like about you," he answered. He stood to his feet and shrugged on his jacket. "If I get an A?" he asked.

"If you get an A," she responded with a smile.

Indie stopped by his house to take a quick shower before he headed to school and as soon as he stepped foot inside he smelled his mother's cooking. He rushed into the kitchen and grabbed a piece of bacon as he kissed his mother's cheek.

"What's up, Ma?" he greeted as he headed up to his room.

"Don't 'what up, Ma' me, Indie Perkins," she said sternly. "Where you been most nights?"

"I been staying at Nanzi's crib," he lied. She knew nothing of his street exploits and she certainly didn't know that he had an apartment in his name where he allowed Parker to reside.

"Lie number one. You tell another one and I'm going to put my foot in your ass," she said.

"I was up late, Ma, studying with a friend," he admitted.

"And the night before that?" she grilled.

"Studying," he shot back.

"Hmm, hmm, studying my ass," she replied. "Why don't you bring her by the house one of these days. I'd like to meet the little fast-tail girl who has my son's nose wide open."

"Never that," he answered. "I'll bring her by, Ma. Don't worry. You'll like her. She's a good girl!" he shouted as he darted up the steps. He showered and swapped clothes before he was back out the door.

School felt so remedial to him. As he walked through the halls everyone around him seemed so much younger than him. Hustling had aged him. He had no interest in the shallow comings and goings of the average high school student. Indie was motivated by paper and, most recently, by Parker. She was the only reason he had even shown up. As he found his way to his class he heard his name being called from the other end of the hall.

"Oh shit, Indie my nigga!"

Indie cringed. Never the one to grandstand Indie would rather fly under the radar than have his presence *announced to the world. He turned to find his friend Bay walking toward him, flaunting a pretty cheerleader type on his arm.*

They slapped hands and embraced briefly as Indie looked left, then right.

"Relax, nigga, you ain't on the block. What's good, baby?" Bay greeted.

"Shit, I'm in and out my nigga. I just came to take this history test," Indie admitted.

"Show up enough to keep moms off your ass?" Bay retorted.

Indie smirked. "Something like that."

Bay reached into his back pocket and pulled out a slip of paper. He handed it to Indie.

"What's this?" he asked.

"The answers to Chatman's test, bro. Thank me later," Bay said. Bay patted him on the back as the first bell rang. "Get with me. I want to talk to you about some real shit."

Indie knew that nothing was for free. Bay had looked out because he wanted Indie to put him on. He could take these answers and get the for-sure A to impress Parker, or he could trust himself and try to accomplish it on his own. He looked up and caught a glimpse of Parker as she made her way down the hall. She didn't even look his way but just the sight of her caused his hand to ball the paper in his hands up. Parker was something that he wanted to earn. If he was going to get her, he didn't want to cheat. This wasn't about the grade. He could feel it in his soul that Parker Banks was supposed to be in his life and as he made his way into his class he realized it was up to him to prove it. He didn't want to hustle his way into her heart and even though school felt like a waste of his time, he wanted to show her that he wasn't a waste of hers.

Chapter 14

Chase slid his finger behind his tie to loosen it a bit as he frowned while stepping on the elevator. *I hate this for show shit,* he thought as he stepped to the back and positioned himself against the wall. On the way to the top floor the elevator would undoubtedly fill and he needed eyes on everyone he shared the short ride with. Vartex Enterprises was one of the leading pharmaceutical companies in the world and now that Indie held a ten percent stake in it they were moving into new territory. "Growth," was what Indie called it, but Chase was a street nigga through and through. It didn't please him to have to get suited just to visit his mans, but he knew that he couldn't jeopardize Indie's new position by coming in looking like riffraff. To even step foot inside the Wall Street corporate monster Chase had to play the part and perfect the role. Even with the monkey suit Chase still stood out like a sore thumb. The color of his skin alone made him feel like an outsider. He could feel the silent stare of curiosity as the men around him wondered how he had even gotten in the building. Indie had stepped his game all the way up. He was about that corporate dollar now and he now had the means to the most potent of prescription pills. He wasn't feeling the new wave that was coming through their camp, simply because it took him out of his element. He was much more comfortable in trap houses and true religions than he was stuffed into the thousand dollar suits. *A nigga barely got room for the burner in this tight shit,* Chase said as he shook his leg while pulling on his pant leg, hoping that the people around him didn't notice the bulge from his nine milli.

As the elevator stopped on each floor, men filed in like sardines, each of them taking a second glance at Chase before turning their backs on him to face the front. When it finally stopped on his floor Chase emerged and made his way to Indie's new office.

"Hi, Mr. . . ."

This nigga got a receptionist and everything, Chase thought as a smirk spread across his face and he cut off the slim brunette who was eyeing him with flirtation in her eyes.

Indie would kill me if I gave her the D.

His thoughts amused him as he stared at the attractive woman intensely. "No mister. You can call me Chase," he said as he held out his hand. The woman shook it softly as her thumb rubbed the top of his hand.

"Nice to meet you, Chase. They are waiting on you," she said.

They? he thought as his brow furrowed in confusion and he followed her into the office. Impressed was an understatement. Indie's new seat on the shareholders board allowed him all of the perks of the company. His office was lavish. Floor-to-ceiling windows gave him the perfect view from the fortieth floor, while all the finest furnishings filled the space inside.

"Mr. Perkins, your final guest has arrived," the woman announced.

Indie nodded and replied, "Thank you, Emma. Please close the door on your way out."

Chase looked at the man who sat across from Indie and immediately stiffened. He didn't welcome strangers easily. Trust was earned in his book and if he didn't fuck with you he didn't fuck with you. Period. He walked up on Indie and embraced him genuinely, giving him the universal sign of love as they slapped hands and then pulled in briefly for a pat on the back. He spoke no words to Indie's guest as he took a seat, scooting his chair over slightly to give himself some space.

"You can put your guard down, fam, this is an associate of mine. Chase, Ethic. Ethic, Chase," he introduced.

Chase shook Ethic's hand reluctantly. He wasn't about the new faces. He trusted Indie wholeheartedly but they were all grown men. Just because Indie rocked with Ethic didn't mean that Chase had to. Ethic would need much more than an introduction to get Chase to lower his guard. He understood the game they were playing in. Many new niggas had been responsible for crumbling drug empires. Hell it was hard to even trust the ones he knew so to accept Ethic with no qualms was damn near impossible.

He wouldn't protest, but he would be extremely careful about the situation in the meantime.

"How did that trip go?" Chase asked.

"Very good," Indie responded. "I called you both here today so that I could acquaint you two and to get the ball rolling. We're moving into pharmaceuticals and Ethic has the means to help us move the product across state lines."

"What about all of our current clientele? If we pull out without notice I can foresee problems," Chase said.

"Niggas don't want my type of problems," Indie replied unfazed.

"Mine either," Ethic added.

"Yeah, I hear you, but I want you to hear me, bro. I get your position. You're in a different place. You have the whole family, wife and kid set-up, big homie, so you need something more than what this coke game has to offer. I'm young and thuggin' it though, fam, and I'm in the streets. I'm in the trap and on the blocks. If we leave the streets dry niggas is going to feel a certain type of way. On top of that you gon' have ten different niggas trying to be the new Scarface of the city. We good money with the hard and soft. From weight to the hand to hands our operation is pumping. These pills, I don't know much about that game. That's that white money. I know how to move bricks but I don't know much about all of this," Chase said as he motioned to the elaborate décor of Indie's office.

"It wouldn't be a bad idea to transition out of cocaine slowly," Ethic said, after weighing Chase's words. "That way things are done peacefully and you have a hand in choosing who takes your reign."

"I've groomed you from day one, Chase. I don't want to make the move into this new realm without you, my nigga. I see the future in this pharmaceutical thing, my baby, and it's bright," Indie said.

"I'm here, bro. Whatever you need. Just don't make me hand over everything I've worked for to the next nigga. You want to appoint a new king at least give me a shot at taking the throne. There's money to be made on all fronts," Chase said.

Indie paused as he sat back in his leather executive chair in deep contemplation. "Get Trina back up here from Houston. Miesha's coming home soon. The three of you will fuck with the coke. Ethic and I will handle the pills. When you're ready to transition you let me know. Eventually I want everyone, all of us, to be on this side of the game. Cocaine is a minority business. Its riskier, more dangerous . . . the Feds are just waiting to lock us all up and we hand 'em the keys by staying in the game long after we should. You get what I'm saying?"

"Absolutely," Chase confirmed. "I'll say good-bye to it before I let it ruin me."

"Smart man," Ethic commented. He stood to his feet and extended love to Indie as they slapped hands. "Let me know when you're ready to move."

He nodded toward Chase in acknowledgment. He felt the cold shoulder and had honestly anticipated it. Young niggas had egos the size of Texas. He remembered that he used to be the same way. "I recognize your gangster, fam, you ain't got to flaunt it. My resume is official though, my nigga. Official," Ethic reiterated seriously, letting Chase know that if it was beef he needed to put it on the table. He turned toward Indie and said, "Chemistry huh?"

Indie nodded, knowing that the team he assembled needed to be just that . . . a team.

"Understood," Indie answered. "Everything's smooth. Just got to work out the kinks between you two mu'fuckas."

"No kinks," Chase spoke up. "Just cautious."

"Why don't we move the setting to something more relaxed? I need both of you to comfortably make this move. I'll have the wife make dinner and we'll all break bread. Sound good?" Indie proposed.

Ethic nodded and made his exit. Once he was gone Chase piped up. "You know how I feel about niggas I'on know, fam," he said. "Fuck this nigga think he is. Ethic? How unoriginal is that shit? He couldn't think of no better name than that? He had to look up a known gangster and bite his shit?"

Indie smirked and replied, "Nah, li'l homie, you got it fucked up. That nigga is 'the' Ethic. No copycat. That's him in the flesh."

The look on Chase's face was priceless and Indie chuckled slightly. "How that foot taste, bro?"

"Man, fuck that nigga!" Chase said jokingly as he laughed too. "Damn, bro, you couldn't warn me or nothing? Fuck! Now I've got to make that shit one hundred next time I see him."

"Nah, you're good. If you hopped in his lap too quickly he wouldn't have respected it. You played it how I would have played it. We good money. Just be there tomorrow night. Tell Miesha. Dinner and drinks and get Trina's ass back to the city too. Fuck she at anyway?"

"She's in Houston. I'll make sure she's around," Chase replied. Indie saw him out and then made his way to his window. He literally sat above the city and being up so high made the game look small. He was about to move into bigger things.

Chapter 15

"Daddy!" Sky's jovial voice filled the house as she ran full speed toward the front door. Like clockwork, whenever she heard keys jiggle in the lock she automatically knew who to expect. YaYa smiled as she moved around the kitchen like a pro. She could have hired a chef to cater the impromptu dinner but cooking relaxed her. It had been so long since she had felt normal that when Indie called her with the idea she happily obliged. She hadn't seen him since he had left for Italy so she hadn't had a chance to inform him of her run-in with Parker. As soon as he had come back into the country he had headed straight to Vartex. Now that he was home and they were expecting guests she didn't think it was the time to address his baby mama drama. YaYa knew one thing, however. She hated Parker and everything she represented. If it hadn't been for Skylar she would have slapped the smug expression off of her face. Yes, a conversation was definitely necessary and it would be had, but not tonight.

"Hey, ma, you miss me?" Indie asked as he appeared in the threshold of the kitchen.

"I did," she replied vaguely as she wrapped her arms around his neck. He leaned down and kissed her lips.

"Do you know how much I love you?" he asked, truly meaning it. His love for her had never been in question. The problem was that he had been tricked out of loving Parker instead of making the choice himself. Now that he knew the truth, that old thing was starting to spark inside of his chest. He had to remind himself to keep the fire at bay. His loyalty was with YaYa or at least he hoped it was. No part of him wanted to hurt her, but it seemed as if life was inevitably delivering pain . . . he just had to decide which woman's doorstep it would be dropped on.

"Indie, we need to talk," she whispered. "Not tonight because I don't want to ruin the mood, but—"

"I know," he said. He kissed her one more time before Skylar ran up to her, hanging on her leg as she squeezed her little body in between them.

"Together!" she screamed happily, melting her parents' hearts.

They shared a family hug and Indie bent to scoop Skylar in her arms. It was one of those moments when everything felt right despite the fact that they were horribly wrong.

Ding! Dong!

The doorbell interrupted them.

"Dinner is ready. I just have to transfer the food to serving dishes. All the guests can start to sit," she said.

"Can you grab the door while I put Skylar down for bed?" he asked.

She nodded and slipped into her Valentino cobalt spiked heels. She removed her apron and placed it atop her kitchen island then smoothed out her designer dress. For the first time she was playing wifey instead of being active in Indie's operation. She wasn't the boss. She wasn't building her power for a plot of revenge. She was simply the hostess, the pretty girl on her man's arm, and it felt good. She couldn't help but wonder how long the feeling would last with Parker in the background playing sabotage. *Fucking bitch,* she thought.

Ding! Dong!

"I've got it, Ma," Indie said, reappearing as he bypassed her and headed toward the door.

"Sorry," she said smiling. "You know I can't be answering doors looking like Aunt Jemima."

He gave her a wink and headed toward the door. She heard Trina's voice as she came toward the kitchen.

"Trina! Where the hell have you been? It's good to see your face finally!" YaYa said.

"It's good to be back," she responded. "I had to get lost for a while. Check on my mom, clear my head."

Trina didn't tell YaYa about the resentment she had built up toward her. In YaYa's pursuit of revenge against Leah, she had thrown a lot of people to the wolves, including Miesha. Miesha had caught a case at YaYa's request. In Trina's mind it was selfish. YaYa was willing to use anyone to get her revenge. She had made her battle everyone's battle and there wasn't anyone that she wouldn't throw under the bus in order to win. Trina loved YaYa dearly, but at the same time she hated her. YaYa was loyal to herself in Trina's eyes. She had a lot of love for Disaya but she wasn't blind to her flaws either.

YaYa looked at Trina curiously, feeling the invisible wall that stood between them. Unbeknownst to Trina, YaYa saw her as a sister. Her selfishness was about survival. She didn't mean to disregard others; it was just the way things were.

"Well I'm glad you're back. Stick around this time, a'ight?" YaYa said with a furrowed brow. She couldn't quite put her finger on it, but something had changed with Trina. She had no idea that Trina's loyalty had wavered long ago. She was in it for the money; it had nothing to do with the family.

"For a little bit," Trina stated. "You need help?" she asked, changing the subject.

"Yeah, you can help me bring all of this food into the dining room," YaYa said.

YaYa grabbed a dish and then made her way toward her formal eating area.

"YaYa, I want to introduce you to someone," Indie said.

YaYa looked up and when she saw his face panic shot through her. A nervous ache pained her heart as she sat the dish down on the table. Ethic. Her knight in shining armor. He was standing here in her home. *What the motherfuck?* she thought. Her mouth opened but no words left it as she was visibly shaken. She had found so much comfort in him and he had crossed her mind many times. His handsome face was just as shocked as her own. He held out his hand as he stared at her curiously, meeting her eyes and making her even more nervous.

"Ethic," he greeted. "It's nice to meet you."

YaYa exhaled, gratefully.

"It's nice to meet you too," she replied. She couldn't break his stare and she was grateful when Miesha came waltzing into the room, loudly making her entrance.

"Hey, everyone!" she greeted.

Indie walked away to greet Miesha but YaYa and Ethic stayed, unmoving.

Despite the fact that nothing happened between them, YaYa felt guilty about their interaction. It wasn't her actions that made her feel disloyal; it was her thoughts, her emotions, her attraction to this stranger.

"YaYa, you need me to do anything?" Miesha asked.

YaYa quickly bypassed Ethic and rounded the table to hug Miesha. She had earned her spot in YaYa's heart and YaYa loved Miesha dearly.

"How are you?" Miesha asked.

YaYa lowered her voice and said, "I could use your help in the kitchen. I'll bet Trina is eating all the food up."

YaYa led Miesha into the kitchen. "Umm, you guys can place the food on the table. I'll be out soon. I'm just going to clean up a little and grab a bottle of champagne," YaYa said.

Trina grabbed another dish and exited, while Miesha sensed something was off.

"YaYa? Are you okay?" Miesha pressed again, this time with a look of genuine concern. The persistency of her questioning told YaYa that her shit wasn't all the way put together. She was letting her slip show, coming unhinged from the stresses that had recently plagued her. "You don't have to be strong all the time. You're not in the game anymore. This isn't a deal and you aren't plotting on anyone. This is your life. Things have been hard for you lately with the wedding and everything . . . I'm just checking on you to make sure you're good. I know what happens when you keep everything to yourself," Miesha said. She then lowered her tone as she continued, "That's how the pill addiction happened last year. I love you. You're the sister I never had. I don't want to see things get that bad again. If you need me I'm here. Ride or die. We can even go stomp that bitch Parker's face in if you want. I got my Tims in the trunk," she said with a laugh.

YaYa laughed because in her younger years that was exactly what she and her old girlfriend Mona would have done. How she had let Miesha get so close she didn't know, but she was slowly realizing that the girl was definitely more than a worker. In fact she was more than a friend. Miesha had become family after proving her loyalty and she appreciated her for the new role that she played in her life. Friends didn't come easily for YaYa. There weren't many women whom she could not only trust, but connect with. Miesha had passed all the tests with flying colors. YaYa's smile was infectious as she replied, "Put your gangster up, girl. The Tims are not needed." She paused. "Yet." She smiled and gave her a wink. "I'm fine, honey, I promise. Go ahead. I'll be out soon."

As soon as YaYa was alone her mind began to spin. *What the hell is Ethic doing here? Is this a game he's playing? Did he know Indie all along?* She poured herself a glass of wine. *I'm going to need this that's for damn sure,* she thought. If she was going to be put in this awkward position you better believe she was going to have a little bit of liquid courage.

She walked back into the dining room and could immediately feel Ethic's eyes on her. It took all of her will not to stare back. The Ferragamo tailored suit he wore was flawless and hung off his muscular frame like the designer had sewn it specifically for him. He was handsome, commanding, and so damn sexy. His serious disposition only added to the mystique. Clearly he was new blood in their crew and he didn't go unnoticed. Trina was definitely interested and YaYa couldn't help but feel a bit of jealousy as Ethic entertained her in conversation. They said grace and then rejoiced in each other's company and feasted like kings. YaYa was quiet most of the dinner as Ethic shared the story of his dealings in the streets with the table. She had heard it just days before, in a much more intimate setting. He was much more vague with the group than he had been with her. She still remembered the passion with which he had spoken when he talked about his son's mother, Raven. She wondered if Indie's love for her emanated off of him whenever he mentioned her name. For some reason, after all that she had put him through she doubted it. She knew that he loved her, but she couldn't help but think that over the struggles over the years he loved her out of routine. That in love, crazy over you, do anything to be with you aspect seemed lost in their relationship and she hadn't noticed it until Indie had hesitated to throw his ex out on their wedding day. *He hesitated,* she thought glumly. *He gave her the upper hand when he chose to speak to her instead of turning around to recite his vows to me.*

That had been one of the most horrid moments of her life. Not even her insane battle with Leah had broken her down as much. Leah's game was mental. She had taken her through psychological and physical hell. Indie had scorned her and targeted straight for the heart. The emotional torture of competing for him and of possibly losing him hurt that much more. Maybe that was what attracted her to Ethic. Ethic wasn't the type to make his woman feel anything less than worthy. Her thoughts were driving her crazy and she had to step away from the table for a while. "I think we need more champagne," she said.

"Do you have wine?" Ethic asked. "Something good."

"She made me build an entire cellar just to store her collection. YaYa appreciates a good, aged bottle of wine," Indie added.

"I'll grab a few bottles," she said.

"I have a 1775 Massandra. Would you like that?" YaYa asked.

Ethic raised an eyebrow. Impressed by her knowledge of good wine.

"That's a fifty thousand dollar bottle. You have good tastes," he complimented. "If you have that in your cellar. I'd love to see what else you have."

"Take him to see it, ma. You know I don't care about all of that. Give me an expensive bottle to pop and I'm good. I'm not with the wine stuff. That talk goes in one ear and out of the other," Indie admitted.

YaYa smirked and then smiled as she stood to her feet. "Follow me," she said to Ethic as they walked through her kitchen and down into the plush basement. She didn't speak to him until they went one more level down into the privacy of the custom-built cellar.

"What the hell are you doing here?" she demanded, finally able to ask. "Did you know I was Indie's fiancée? Were you using me to try to get in good with him?"

Ethic smiled slightly.

"Oh you find this funny? This is my life. I don't know what kind of bullshit games you're playing . . ."

Ethic closed the space between them, pushing her back against one of the shelves of wine. "You're sad . . . tell me why."

She exhaled as she shook her head. *How is he able to read me so well?* she thought. *He doesn't even know me.*

"I can't do this. You being here is awkward," she said.

"Don't avoid my question. Why are you still sad?" he pushed.

Tears came to YaYa's eyes. "He has a son. I saw him with my own eyes. I feel like some random girl that I didn't even know a week ago is going to come in and steal my life," she admitted as she lowered her head in despair. Ethic was the only person who felt her pain. He was the only one who it was easy to talk to.

"If she can steal him, let her have him, ma," Ethic said as he lifted her chin and stared her in the eyes. There was something about the way he looked at her. It was electric and made every nerve in her body feel alive. "His inability to see what he has in front of him just may bless the next man," Ethic said.

"How are you here?" she asked as he wiped away the stray tear that had escaped her.

"This isn't a set-up, ma. I don't play those games. I met Indie through a mutual friend. We're in business together. I didn't know you were his girl until I stepped foot inside this house. I never thought I would see you again, but I can't say I'm disappointed," Ethic said. "And for the record, my name is all the weight I need in the game. Indie is that nigga in New York, but there's a whole world out there, ma. My name holds weight alone. I would never use a man's woman to align myself with anyone. Remember that," he said.

They stood so closely that YaYa could smell the sweet smell of his breath and feel his lips touching hers slightly as he spoke. Here, in the depths of the cellar, she felt completely connected to him and the moisture building between her legs was unstoppable.

Nothing but pure adulation pulsed between them as the lovely tension in the room caused neither of them to walk away.

"If he leaves, let him," Ethic whispered. For a moment she thought he would kiss her, but instead he reached over her and grabbed a bottle of wine off of the rack. He adjusted his suit and turned to walk out and rejoin the crowd, leaving YaYa breathless from their interaction.

"Yo, did she show you the cellar?" Indie asked as Ethic reentered the dining room.

"Indeed, it's like a vineyard down there. She's quite the connoisseur," Ethic said as he reclaimed his seat.

"Tell me about it, that shit costs me a fortune," Indie cracked as he felt his phone vibrate in the breast pocket of his Gucci suit. He retrieved it and his smile slowly faded as he read the words.

> Tell your bitch of a "wife" that I'm not some cheap whore. She can't bribe me or my son out of your life. I don't need her dirty money and I'm starting to think that maybe King and I don't need you.
> —Parker

The text message popped up on Indie's screen, assaulting him without warning. He had no idea what Parker was talking about but he knew exactly who to ask. He had just been having the time of his life, breaking bread and popping bottles with his people over the prosperity to come. Now, his entire mood had gone dark. He could never imagine YaYa propositioning Parker to leave town, but he knew that his judgment on her integrity was not always on point. She had done much worse in her day. "Excuse me," he said as he pressed call in an attempt to calm Parker. He could hear her practically screaming at him through her texts. The tone of her words bit at his conscience as his anger sparked.

He clenched his strong jaw as he went in search for YaYa. He found her just as she was coming out of the wine cellar carrying a bottle of vintage Merlot in her hands.

"What did you do, ma?" he asked calmly, startling her.

She jumped, clasping her chest as she exhaled. "Sneak up on people much?" she asked playfully as she calmed her racing heart.

"Fuck did you do, Disaya?" he asked, this time raising his voice slightly.

YaYa's eyes widened as she stood taken aback. He never, ever called her by her real name. She couldn't even remember the last time she had heard it fall off of his lips.

"Nothing, what are you talking about?" she asked, defensively, thinking that maybe Ethic had lied to her and was here to throw shade about their one night spent together. "Nothing happened."

Indie chuckled sarcastically as his temper began to flare. "Nothing happened? Then explain this!" he demanded as he tossed the phone her way.

She caught it and picked it up, dumbfounded as to why he was so angry. When she read the text message she quickly found out. She didn't give a damn about what he was talking about. Only one thing rang in her mind.

"Why is she texting you? Huh? Why do the bitch even have your number?" YaYa barked, now seeing red right along with him. She knew the answers to all of her questions. Parker had his son. They had things to figure out. Of course she had his number, but still it bothered YaYa.

"She has my fucking son!" Indie shouted, frustrated.

"I don't give a fuck about your son!" YaYa countered. "So what? You two just sit up and text and call each other all day? She taking you on a glorious stroll down memory lane and you falling for it? That bitch ruined our wedding day and you said nothing to her! You didn't check her about it, you didn't tell her to kick rocks . . . but I go to handle the situation and get her out of our lives and you try to jump bad at me?" YaYa was on a roll. She could say a million things before she ever let Indie get a word in. "So what I offered her money to leave town? The bitch better be glad I didn't sic wolves on her ass!" YaYa barked. "I did what you wouldn't!"

"I was handling it!" he countered.

"How?" she shouted. "By making secret trips to her hotel room at The London?"

The guilty look on his face only added fuel to her fire. "You left the key in your pants pocket."

"It's not what you think, but what do you want from me?" Indie asked. "She is here and she isn't going anywhere. She has my son that I have yet to meet. He might not even be mine, but—"

"Oh shut up!" YaYa said. "He's yours! I saw him with my own eyes. He's your son," she said as tears came to her eyes. "I know it was before me but it doesn't stop me from being afraid of losing you. You're sneaking off to see this girl! Texting her obviously! Tell me what's real, Indie, not what you think I want to hear! Do you still have feelings for this girl?"

Indie lowered his head and didn't reply, but silence sounded so much like a resounding yes.

"You want to know the real, ma? The real is right now I've got to go fix what you fucked up. I can't let Parker leave town with my son. I missed so many years. Right now I don't know what I feel, but the shit you pulled . . . it was foul, YaYa."

Indie turned and stormed up the steps, leaving her boiling with so much rage and hurt that she thought it may destroy her.

She made her way back up the steps, embarrassed, because at the volumes that she and Indie had been battling she was sure that her guests had heard everything. An awkward silence filled the room as soon as she stepped back in. At first she sought words to explain but then she waved her hand in dismissal. She wasn't explaining or lying to cover up what they had just witnessed. Fuck it. They had heard it. Hell they had seen it at the wedding. There was a bitch threatening to replace her. "Just leave," she whispered. She turned and walked up the stairs, feeling completely empty.

She made her way to Skylar's room and was grateful to find that she was still sleeping peacefully. She vowed that no matter how much of a struggle that she was going through, she would never let Skylar's life feel anything less than normal again. She had gone through enough behind her parents' messy lives. YaYa was still trying to make up for her past transgressions as a mother. She wanted to be more attentive and to provide a safe, loving home for her child. With Indie's focus divided between two families, she was slowly realizing that while she was a full-time mom, he may only be able to commit to being a half-time dad. That alone saddened her.

Wine, it's a cheesecake and wine type of night, she thought. She knew that her favorite design paired with a complementing drink would keep her from crying her eyes out the remainder of the night. YaYa had a vindictive soul; that much had been proven over the years by her relentless efforts to kill Leah's ass. Part of her wanted to destroy Parker, hell maybe even Indie's wishy-washy ass. He didn't know where he wanted to be. How could this even be an issue? When it came down to it he was supposed to pick her! No doubts and no hesitation. Since he was acting brand new she wanted too as well, but she didn't want to make permanent decisions on temporary emotions.

She went into her bathroom and showered, washing the makeup from her face, letting the salty tears mix with the steaming hot water. Usually this routine soothed her soul, but today when the stakes were so high it did very little. She stepped out, leaving small puddles on the tile where she walked as she headed into her bedroom. Slipping into a long silk robe that complemented her silhouette she headed down to the kitchen. The sound of clanging dishes caused her to frown. *I thought I told everyone to leave,* she thought in irritation, not wanting to be bothered. She entered the kitchen and she saw Ethic loading her dishes into a sink full of soapy water.

Voila. Just like magic the sight of him instantly made her hurt disappear. She had to admit that she was feeling him in a real way. What at first she thought she could avoid was now a fixture in her life. He was going to be around and she wasn't sure if she could handle it. Every time they interacted he made her feel as if she were made of gold.

"What are you doing?" she asked as she walked over to him. She dipped her hands into the sink.

"You wash, I dry?" Ethic asked with a smile.

"Where they make you at? I can't pay my nigga to wash dishes around here," she said with a slick smile.

"I think it's very obvious after tonight that your nigga ain't built like me," Ethic replied.

She began to wash and rinse then handed them to Ethic to dry and put them away.

"You do know I have a dishwasher right?" she asked playfully.

"This gives me an excuse to be here. I'd rather do this slow," he answered.

"So that's how you like it?" she said, surprised by her own flirting.

He smirked.

"Thank you for staying," YaYa said. "I thought I needed to be alone, but your company always makes everything seem better."

"I hate that every time I see you, you have the same look in your eyes," he said as he dried the last dish. He dried his hands with the same towel as she turned to him.

"What look is that?" she asked.

"Sadness."

Tears. Those damn raindrops full of emotion that she had no control over flooded her again. She felt the downpour threatening to fall and she hated the fact that she was so transparent.

"How is it that you see right through me?" she asked.

"I pay attention," he answered. He noticed her phone sitting on the kitchen island and he picked it up and dialed his own number so that it was stored in her recent calls. "I'm headed back to Flint soon, but if you ever need anything all you have to do is call, you understand. Anything, ma." He graced her cheek lovingly and YaYa rested her face in the palm of his hand as she closed her eyes. She didn't even realize that they had moved closer for a kiss until her lips were already touching his. She knew that she should pull away or stop herself, but she couldn't and most importantly she didn't want to. The way her heart raced and the feel of his strong embrace as he wrapped a hand around her waist to pull her near all felt too good. Their chemistry was amazing and for that moment he was the glue that welded her heart back together.

He pulled away first and shook his head as he stared at her. "This is messy. I'm in business with your man," he said, already kicking himself for allowing YaYa to get to him.

"We can't do this," she whispered as she wiped her lips delicately with her thumb as if she could remove the traces of their kiss. "You should go." The ultimate heartbreak resounded in her voice as she watched him turn away. She wasn't sure exactly what she was doing or feeling but it was familiar. She remembered what it felt like to fall for someone, but how could she be falling for Ethic when she already had Indie? The problem was she didn't know that she still had Indie. He had left doubt and given her room to think that he was loyal somewhere else. Indie had left just enough space for a refined gangster like Ethic to step in and show her the type of loyalty she craved.

She heard Ethic reach the door as he clicked the lock. "Ethic!" she yelled. She ran out of the kitchen and he turned to her as she ran into his arms. This time their kiss was undeniable as their tongues danced sensuously. His hands roamed everywhere. Palming her ass, tracing the contour of her body through the robe, finally gripping the back of her neck. He held her like he never wanted to let go. He made her feel like maybe, just maybe, there could be love after Indie. They pulled away from one another before they took things too far. They both were eager, wanting, but neither was ready to take it to that level. Ethic knew how it felt to fuck with YaYa would be love and war. He was ready to spark beef over someone else's chick. In the end he knew that she was too in love with Indie to choose him. If she was ever given the chance, YaYa would repair her family. She wasn't ready to leave; she just wanted to feel loved. It was because of that fact that he had to walk away.

"Take care of yourself," he said.

"You too," she answered. As soon as she closed the door she put her back against the wall and slid to the floor.

She had no idea what she was feeling but now more than ever before she was confused. She didn't know what she wanted. She was just lost.

Chapter 16

Parker and Indie's past

Knock! Knock!

Parker made her way to the door, cautiously peeking out of the peephole just to be safe. When she saw Indie's face she frowned. He never visited her this early in the day and she knew he wasn't delivering any dough because he hadn't yet hit the block. She pulled open the door.

"Hey," she greeted with an unsure smile. "What's going on? What are you doing here?"

"I've got something for you," he said. He handed her an envelope.

"What is this? An eviction notice or something?" she asked sarcastically. She opened the letter and smiled in shock. Before she could say anything Indie picked her up, tossing her over his shoulder as he made his way across the threshold.

"I got an A, baby girl!" he said excitedly.

"Aghh!" she screamed playfully as he spun her around. She laughed as he placed her on her feet and he kissed her passionately. She didn't stop him. Hey, a deal was a deal. She had promised him that he could take her out if he got an A on his exam, but she had a better idea. She wanted to stay in. She returned his efforts, pressing her body against his as she reached down and pulled his shirt over her head.

She loved everything about Indie, but he was everything that was no good for her. She needed him on her page. They had to be focused on the same things if he wanted her to trust her heart in his hands.

"Wait," she said, pulling away as her chest heaved up and down lustfully.

"What's wrong?" he asked.

"I'm so proud of you for getting the A. You did what I always knew you could do, but what does this mean? What does it change?" she asked.

Exasperated Indie swiped his face. "What you want from me, P?"

"I want you to say that this A leads to more A's. That if I give you what I've given no other guy that you won't play me. I want you to be worthy of it and I can't lie, Indie, a nigga that's on the block day and night isn't worthy of it. I don't want to be that girlfriend, wondering if you're going to come home or not. I don't want to go away to college in a year and leave you behind because you're focused on the streets. If you want to do this I'm down, but I'm not the girl that wants to be the dopeman's wife. That's not cool to me. Indie, you're smart," she said as she cupped his face. "You can be a doctor or a lawyer or an entrepreneur. You're so much more than the streets," she said.

Indie let her go and went to his backpack.

"You're leaving?" she asked, hoping that she hadn't offended him.

He pulled a half a brick out of his bag and grabbed her by the elbow as he practically dragged her to the bathroom.

"Indie! What are you doing?" she asked as he lifted the lid of the toilet. He ripped a hole in the package and began to flush the product away. "Indie!" she shouted in shock.

When he was done he balled up the empty plastic and flushed that as well. He turned toward Parker and asked, "I'ma be whatever you want me to be, P. If you want a college boy, I'll be that. I don't know if my grades are good enough to get accepted to those fancy colleges you applying for, but I'll try. If I can't get into Howard, I'll go to the community college nearby while you take classes at the university. Whatever you want, I'll be that and if this isn't it, I'll give it all up," Indie said, pouring his young heart out.

She rushed him, wrapping her arms around his neck. "I think I just fell in love with you," she whispered.

"I know I love the shit out of you, ma," he replied. "I just have one request."

She frowned. "What's that?"

"You've got to meet my moms. She not too pleased with all of the time you've been taking up," he said. "But when she meets you, she'll understand. She'll love you because I love you and you're doing what she hasn't been able to."

"What's that?" Parker asked.

"You're getting her baby boy out of the streets," he replied.

Parker smiled as she thought of the day Indie came running to her apartment to claim her heart. He had not only walked away with her loyalty that day, but her virginity as well. *I was so in love with him,* she thought. To many people, their love was simply a phase, puppy love, and something to be discounted, but it was the strongest bond she had ever felt. That first time you felt something real with a man who saw the world in the same shade as you . . . it was unforgettable. She hadn't had the pleasure of feeling anything even close to that ever since.

"Ma, it's your move," King said, snapping her out of her daydreams. She grabbed the dice to the Monopoly board and was about to toss them when the doorbell to the suite chimed off.

"Did you order something, boo bop?" she asked, calling her son the nickname that she had used since birth.

"Ma! I don't like it when you call me that!" he griped.

She chuckled and shook her head as he blushed. Her baby boy was truly not a baby anymore. He was growing into quite the young man lately. She pulled open the door without thinking twice and Indie's face immediately made her heart drop into her stomach.

The anguish he wore on his face melted her anger into confusion, into love. All she wanted to do was pull him into her arms, but her stubborn Leo nature caused her to keep her poker face intact. "Did you send her over here to do your bidding?" she asked, crossing her arms and blocking him from entering.

"No, ma. I would never. You disappearing from my life again is the last thing I want," he admitted. There was nothing but sincerity in his words.

"Ma, come on! It's your turn!" King called out from inside the suite.

Indie's eyes widened. "He's here?" he asked, with a mixture of nerves and excitement causing inflation in his tone.

She nodded. "He is."

"Can I meet him?" Indie asked.

Parker paused. For so long she had been the barrier of protection between her child and the hurt that the world had to offer. Letting Indie in would be like putting a slow leak in the tire. She was about to rock King's world with the introduction to his father. A part of her didn't want to, but she knew that it wasn't her place to keep a father from his son. That was a bond that she would never understand

and could never mimic, so instead she stuck up a warning finger. "If you hurt my son, I will fucking ruin your life, Indie Perkins," she said with fire in her eyes as her voice trembled, emotionally.

"I believe you," he said with a smile. She stepped to the side and allowed Indie to walk into the room.

She closed the door and then led him to the living area where her son sat over the game board. "King, baby, I want you to meet your dad," she managed.

Neither Indie or King moved, but instead they stared at one another unsure of how to react. Indie's eyes watered because he was literally looking into himself. King was a replica of Indie. Elaine had pictures lined up on a mantel that looked as though the child before him had posed in them.

Indie looked back at Parker, unsurely, but she looked just as lost as the two of them. He turned and swiped his hand over his head as he blew out a deep breath. "How you doing, man?" Indie asked.

"I'm G," King answered.

Indie couldn't help but chuckle as Parker shook her head while rolling her eyes in amusement. King had poked out his chest a little more than usual, put a bit more bass in his voice. Words like gangster, G, he had never used them before, but he was obviously trying to prove himself.

"I'm glad I finally got the chance to meet you, King," Indie said.

"Where you been?" King asked.

Indie sighed as he wondered how he was going to explain this circumstance without pointing fingers. "I didn't know about you, King. Your mom had a hard time getting in contact with me, but she finally found me and now that I've met you, I hope you'll still give me a chance to be around. That cool with you?"

King chewed on his bottom lip and fiddled with his fingers as he thought it over. Indie had never felt so much heat in his life. His son, his mini-me, was sitting back debating about whether he wanted to know him or not. Indie's heart was beating out of his chest.

"What kind of car you drive?" King asked.

Indie laughed. "I've got a couple, li'l man."

"What's your favorite?" King countered.

Indie turned to Parker again and she shrugged and said, "Answer the man!"

"My Phantom is a'ight," Indie replied.

"You got a Phantom? You must be rich!" King exclaimed.

"Must be," Indie replied, amused.

"You can teach me how to be rich when I grow up?" King asked.

"It's in your veins, li'l homie. You're going to shoot to the top," Indie assured. "Now what you think? Can we do this father and son thing?" Indie extended his hand for a shake.

"Yeah, I'm cool with that!" King exclaimed excitedly, shaking his father's hand. "You can take Mama's turn. She's no competition."

Parker put her hands on her hip and cocked her head to the side. "Hey!" she frowned.

"You can be the banker, ma," Indie said with a wink.

He removed his leather jacket and laid it over the couch as he took a seat. Parker got on her knees as she leaned over the board and King made it a point to sit directly next to Indie. His heart warmed as he made eye contact with Parker. *This is what family feels like,* he thought. As he looked at his son and the woman with whom he had created him, Indie realized that this was the vision that he had imagined when he was younger. This right here was all he had ever wanted.

They stayed up for hours until Parker regretfully had to bring the night to a close. "All right, King, it's time for bed, boo bop," she said.

"Maybe now that I've got a dad you can tell her to stop calling me that," King complained as he stood to his feet.

"Yeah, I think you're right. We can come up with something a little more G than that," Indie said as he rubbed King's head and pulled him in for a hug. King hugged him tightly and then ran to Parker, giving her the world's biggest hug.

As he kissed her cheek he whispered, "Thanks, Ma, he's way better than my friends' dads."

She watched him walk into the second bedroom of the penthouse and then turned to Indie.

"That was easier than I thought it would be," she said, sounding relieved.

She bent down to pick up the pieces of the game but Indie grabbed her arm overcome with emotion and pulled her into him. He kissed her gently pouring out his gratitude into her. Parker's body bowed as she leaned into him. "Come home, Indie," she whispered. "Just be with us."

He knew that it was wrong, but sometimes wrong felt right and when right was all wrong, confusion sent reason out of the window. He was acting off of emotion, taking directions from his heart. It was the only thing he trusted at the moment. He picked her up, scooping her legs from beneath her, their lips never breaking contact as he entered the master bedroom.

He wanted to be the man to walk away from the temptation, but it wasn't his loins that was urging him forward . . . it was his heart. The chemistry between them had gone nowhere over the past eight years. If anything, absence had made them fonder of one another. She moaned, completely captive at his touch as he peeled her out of her clothes. His flesh pressed into her through the fabric of his slacks. Within moments they were naked. Skin to skin. Eye to eye. Chest to chest. The moment overwhelmed the both of them. Not another person in the world existed right now. Not YaYa, not Elaine and her meddling ways. This was their time and as Indie eased her onto the bed he lifted one leg until it dangled over his shoulder. He kissed her calf as he entered her. She gasped as he filled her. When she had run away she had left a boy behind, but Indie was all man now. As he bowed in and out of her succulence she matched his stroke aggressively. Their bodies intertwined like most intricate puzzle as they switched from position to position. From the bed, to the floor. He even hit her from the back as her breasts pressed against the floor-to-ceiling windows, overlooking the sparkling lights to the city. Making up for lost time, they peaked numerous times, until exhaustion willed them to throw in the towel. As they got in the shower Indie looked her in the eyes and said, "Thank you for my son."

"You're welcome," she whispered. "Where do we go from here?" she asked.

There it was. Reality. Her words reminded him that life was waiting on him outside of the bedroom door. YaYa. Skylar. He lowered his head against her forehead as tension filled him. He loved YaYa, but he loved Parker as well. Now that he had met his son and Parker had opened her heart to him he couldn't see himself living without her again. Then again, how could he live without YaYa? He had tried to let her go before only to realize that without her by his side a sizable void existed in his life. His dilemma was heavy. There was no right response.

"I don't know," he replied. "I need you to promise me that you won't leave again. There isn't a day that I don't want to be in your life . . . in King's life. When I saw him, I felt whole. King is like a do over for me. It's a chance to watch myself grow up all over again, this time I get to stop him from making all of the mistakes though. I need him. I need you."

Parker kissed his lips. "You have us, but we won't be your best kept secret."

"I'd never ask you to be," Indie said.

Parker stepped out of the shower and wrapped herself in a towel. "Hurry up so I can see you out. My eyes feel like they are on fire. You've put me to sleep," she said.

"See me out?" Indie asked as he rinsed and stepped out, grabbing the towel she was extending to him. He wrapped it around his waist.

"Absolutely," she answered. "You can't stay the night. King has never seen any man coming out of my bedroom. I don't do that and until I know for sure what this is between us, he won't see you laying up either. I want my son to respect me therefore you have to leave."

"I respect it," he answered. He dressed quickly and headed for the door. "I'll be by tomorrow."

She looked at him with doubt.

"Every day, he'll see my face," he said. He kissed her one last time, unable to resist. "Good night, P."

"Good night."

Chapter 17

YaYa sat back in the rocking chair, gently swaying as Skylar slept soundly in her arms. Usually it was a mother's job to comfort her child, but tonight it was Skylar's presence that was soothing YaYa's soul. The unconditional love of her child gave her just the amount of support she needed to say "fuck you" to Indie. As long as she had Sky she didn't need him. Fuck it. Or at least that's what she tried to convince herself of. The minutes ticked by torturously slow as she anticipated Indie's arrival. He had stayed out all night, which was uncharacteristic of him. Sleeping outside of their home was just something that they didn't do. It was a deal breaker. YaYa wasn't a naïve girl. Before falling for Indie, she was the type who thought all men cheated. As long as it didn't come back to her she never tripped, but meeting him had changed her perspective. She had fallen so deeply in love with Indie that she had let love blind her. She had let Indie make her believe that maybe just maybe fairytales did exist. That's why this sudden betrayal stung so badly. She hadn't seen it coming and now that he was suddenly switching up it made her feel as if she might die. She had called Indie's phone so many times that she started to call herself crazy. Each time she got his voicemail. She left no message simply because she knew that she would spew hate in his inbox, which may cause him to stay away even longer. A part of her only wanted him to come home just so that she could pop off. So much animosity sat on the tip of her tongue that it burned. She couldn't wait to see his face. She had an entire monologue ready to go for that ass as soon as he crossed over the threshold. For him to have the audacity to walk out on her in front of their friends while announcing that he was going to see Parker had pushed her over the edge. First the embarrassment of their incomplete wedding, now this. Nah . . . YaYa wasn't feeling that nigga at all and she was about to let it be known. The complacency of an established relationship often made people forget who they were really dealing with. She had played the back for too long and Indie had forgotten about the feisty diva that she had been before he had tamed her. He was about to learn today . . . if he ever came home, that was.

YaYa was so upset that she didn't even feel guilty about kissing Ethic. What normally would have made her feel like the worst person in the world now felt well deserved. The only thing that bothered her about the kiss was that she couldn't keep her mind off of it. Her lips still tingled where his had touched. She had been with Indie for a long time . . . so long that she had forgotten what it felt like to be wanted by anyone else. Ethic was a boss of a man. The things that he had been through had matured him to the point where he played no games when it came to life or matters of the heart. As badly as she wanted to explore the feelings that she felt, the last thing she wanted to do was use him as a rebound just to make herself feel better. She had reached for her phone to call him many times throughout the night, but she always stopped herself. The things that she felt for that man when he looked in her eyes scared her. She didn't even know him, but she was almost certain that if ever given the chance he would steal her heart away from Indie. She wasn't ready for that and she knew it.

The familiar sound of Indie's car could be heard as he pulled into the driveway. She stood as her heart skipped a beat. Placing Skylar gently in her bed she walked to the stairs and stood at the top of them, waiting for Indie to enter the front door.

Now that he was home her anger had diminished into sadness because she knew the revelation that was about to be revealed. Indie had never been a liar and she knew that once she asked him the inevitable question he would provide the inevitable truth. A man didn't stay out all night doing nothing at all. He hadn't feared the consequences of not coming home because Parker had made it worth it for him to stay. YaYa's heart ached as it thundered in her chest and as soon as she saw Indie's face tears filled her eyes.

She didn't even need an admission of guilt. Women were territorial and she could practically smell Parker's scent on her man. It didn't matter that he had washed away the evidence. Indie had given what belonged to her, away. The sting of his betrayal immediately turned love to hate. She hated him for being so weak. Fidelity wasn't easy. It was a choice and he had made his that night. This was the pivotal point where most women got it wrong. In this moment she had to decide to stay or leave him. If she stayed, Indie would never respect her and his transgressions would be repetitive because her staying was the same as her accepting that this is how their life was going to be. Nope. Not happening. YaYa wasn't that bitch. She would take her green-eyed, five foot seven inch, magnificently sculpted, pretty ass to a man who could keep his dick where it belonged.

Just to see if he would lie to her she asked, "You fucked her right?"

Indie hadn't seen this type of hurt in YaYa's eyes since he had left her years ago to move to Houston. There was

no sparkle in her beautiful gaze, no light in her face. He
had murdered her spirit. Disappointment and devastation filled him as he realized the error of his ways. His
anger toward her had led him right into Parker's bed. He
had wronged her but he was so lost that he didn't know
how to get it right. He truly loved both women. What was
a man to do? He stepped toward her, wrapping his hand
around her waist. "I'm sorry," he whispered.

YaYa pushed him away, but he pulled her closer again
as his own tears came to him. He could feel them breaking
up. He could feel the crack that would split their lives in
half, making her withdraw from him forever. It hurt. "I'm
sorry, ma," he said as he tried to hug her. She couldn't
withhold the emotion that fell from her eyes. She pushed
him. "I'm sorry, ma. I'm so sorry. I need you."

She writhed at his touch and fought against him as he
held her tightly in a bear hug, refusing to her go.

"Let go of me," she cried.

"Please don't leave me, YaYa. I love you. I'm sorry," he
pleaded as his tears fell and she pulled away from him.

Smack!

Her hand flew across his face full force. "Don't fucking
touch me. Fuck you and your 'I'm sorry.' You fucked her,
Indie!" she shouted at the top of her lungs. She went
upstairs and grabbed Skylar out of her bed, making sure
to wrap the covers around her sleeping toddler. Indie was
hot on her heels.

"Don't say shit to me," YaYa growled. "You made your
choice. Now I'm making mine."

Her bags were already packed and tucked away in the
trunk of her car. Indie pulled at her. "Wait a minute!
You're not leaving me. YaYa, baby, wait a minute," Indie
said, desperate for her to hear him out, despite the fact
that he had no defense. There was no excusing his actions
yet he still pleaded. He didn't care how weak he sounded

because he knew that once she walked out of the door that it would be next to impossible to repair what had been broken.

"What about all the times I forgave you?" he asked as he put his hands on his head in distress, while watching her place his daughter safely in the back seat.

"You shouldn't have. I wouldn't have. You only get one time to show me who you really are. Now that I see, I believe you." She shut the door and opened the garage as she pulled away. The sight of Indie dropping to his knees in dismay almost made her change her mind, but when she thought of him doing the things to Parker that he did to her, she pressed her feet harder on the gas pedal. *Bitch-ass nigga,* she thought in disgust as she skirted away from what was once her home. The farther away she drove the more tears blurred her vision. She couldn't believe that less than a few weeks ago she was planning her wedding to the man that she loved; now she was plotting her escape from the man that she hated. It was a shame that they were one and the same.

Chapter 18

"Tell me again why you still fuck with YaYa after she sent you upstate on a dummy mission? You could have gotten fucked up while being locked down. The shit happens every day. A bitch will go to jail over some petty shit like shoplifting and fuck around and catch a murder charge while they're there. You don't watch the news? You ain't hear about that Red Bottom Bandits bitch that got caught up! On her release day, one of them hating-ass bitches up in there tried to kill her but the chick Raegan ended up fighting her up off her. The fight was so bad she ended up throwing the girl over some railing to her death. Now chick is facing life on a murder rap. Tell me that couldn't have been you?" Trina yapped as they waited for their business associates to arrive.

"I never said it couldn't have been me. It just wasn't me. Now shut up with all that. Here they come," Miesha said as she hopped out of the tinted Tahoe and hit the button to lift the gate in the back to show an empty trunk. Guns had never been their game, but Chase wanted more firepower if he was going to expand. With Indie handing over the reins to a lucrative cocaine empire there would be much opposition to the throne. He wanted to be prepared. He didn't trust outsiders and wouldn't be eager to add numbers to the team, so instead he needed to add numbers to his arsenal. He needed to let the opposition that was threatening to rise know that he would pull out the choppers if their silent protests got too loud. He sent

Miesha and Trina to make the exchange. $50,000 worth of guns on the street was enough to fight any pending war.

The pretty faces that he sent on his behalf were easily underestimated, but they held their own. They had been thugging it since they were teenagers. Starving at the bottom, they were more than eager to prove themselves when Indie had first given them the opportunity to earn their keep. From cook-up queens, to highway runs, and recently enforcers, they had always gotten the job done. The older Trina got she realized that there was a price to pay, however. They were the sacrificial lambs, the pawns to the game. She was feeling it, but Miesha on the other hand was sitting back pretty. For the work she had put in for YaYa she had a nest egg put up that would guarantee her and her family's future. She didn't even have to live the life anymore. She was in it out of loyalty and for the feeling of being a part of something powerful. The money at this point was an extra.

The girls stood attentively as they watched three Puerto Rican men exit the Chevy van.

Trina and Miesha met the men halfway between the vehicles.

"You must be Eduardo," Trina said.

"You're definitely not Chase, *mami*," the man replied. He wore a jean jacket, bare chest underneath with leather pants. His arms, neck, and face were covered in tattoos. The average chick may have been intimidated, but Trina showed nothing of the sort.

"Chase sits on a new throne. The streets won't see him as much. You'll see my pretty ass a lot though so let's get the bullshit out the way right now. Don't let my skirt fool you. We'll make this quick and painless every time. Strictly business. You get your money, we get our guns. You got me?" she asked.

"*Sí, mamacita,* I got you," he answered. "You got the money?" he asked.

"You got my fucking guns? I'm not buying anything blind," she countered.

"They're in the van," he said.

He turned and walked them to the back of his vehicle. Miesha stepped back while Trina leaned down to peek into the oversized black duffels. As she bent her eyes met the eyes of the driver who was watching her nervously through the rearview mirror. Beads of sweat were dripping into his dancing eyes and a cold shiver ran straight through Trina. Something was off and she felt it. She closed her eyes as everything seemed to play out in slow motion. She had let these niggas she didn't know walk her to the edge of her grave. *Fuck!* she thought. *These niggas are about to rob me.* In this business robbing was always followed by murder. There was no way he would leave her alive. "I forgot to tell you I don't have all the money," she said, trying to distract Eduardo as she reached into one of the bags and quickly loaded the clip of one of the pistols. If she didn't have the money maybe it wouldn't be worth it to go through with his plans to double cross her. Or perhaps he would kill her anyway for wasting his time.

Miesha frowned because the money was tucked in her waistline securely. She didn't have time to ponder and she was a shoot first ask questions kind of girl. She drew on Eduardo instantly.

Boom!

His brains splattered all over Trina but she didn't hesitate as she pulled the gun out of the duffel and popped one in the driver's head, while Miesha quickly put two in the chest of the third man.

Rattled, Trina grabbed one of the duffels and tossed it to Miesha. She could feel Eduardo's brains and blood as it dried on the back of her neck and she cringed.

"What the fuck?" Miesha asked as they ran back to their own vehicle.

"Thank God you're my bitch! If you hadn't popped off that would be us over there," Trina said, as tears of relief built in her eyes.

"How do you know?" Miesha asked.

"I just know," Trina answered.

As she sped away from the scene Trina knew that she wasn't going to continue to risk her life. She was tired of being a shooter and definitely tired of New York. It wasn't her territory and she set it in her mind that day she was headed back to Houston, sooner rather than later.

"How did it go, bad?" Indie asked as he stood over Trina and Miesha as they sat at the table.

"Your people were not there to make a fucking deal," Trina said. "If we didn't do what we did, we wouldn't be sitting here right now. Your people were dirty."

"I've been dealing with them for years," Indie stated. "Do you know whose son that was? It'll be problems."

"Then let it be problems," Chase said. "No offense, fam, but you're out of this game. You let me take the reins and that makes me accountable. It's my mess, let me clean it up."

Indie nodded. It was instinctive for him to take control, but he would have to be hands-off in order to keep his business with Vartex intact. He would have to trust Chase to take care of the street side of things. "Just make sure that you don't get cleaned up in the process. The Dominicans don't take disrespect lightly. Don't underestimate anyone."

"I never do," Chase replied.

***

Ethic pulled his G-Class Mercedes truck up to the warehouse and flashed his lights to let Indie know that it was him. His eighteen-wheeler had already arrived and the driver was helping to load the "inventory" onto the back of his truck. He shut off his engine and exited the vehicle as Indie approached him.

"I wasn't expecting you, fam," Indie said as they slapped hands.

"It's the first run. I needed to make sure everything went smoothly on my end. No hiccups," he stated.

Indie nodded as he gave Ethic a firm pat on the back. "My man," he said. "Come on in, I'll show you how I'm sending the crates." They entered the warehouse that was illuminated in yellow lights that hung from the fifty-foot ceilings.

"Being on the board of Vartex has its perks. I have access to any drug we manufacture," Indie stated. He picked up a crow bar that lay on the ground and pried open one of the wooden crates. Bottles and bottles of prescription pills were stacked neatly inside. "I bust open the bottles and transfer them into bean bags. It will take the dogs to sniff out this and on a routine police stop that will never happen. If any of your drivers get pulled over and searched, all the police will find is bean bags that are being shipped to toy stores all over the US. They'll never know that the pills are really what's stuffed inside."

"Looks like we're good money," Ethic replied. Their operation was damn near flawless and he could already see the paper stacking in his safe. As he looked at Indie his thoughts drifted to YaYa. He hadn't spoken to her since the disastrous dinner party but she had crossed his mind like she was his favorite song, playing on repeat. "How did that other thing work out?" he asked.

"What's that?" Indie asked.

"Things with wifey got kind of heated at your little gathering. We need your head clear if we're going to do square business," Ethic probed. He could care less about Indie; he really wanted to find out what was up with YaYa. She was interesting and certainly beautiful to say the least.

"Shit's messy, but that's neither here nor there. Nothing is going to get in the way of this money. We're good," Indie replied.

"Hey, boss, this load is ready to go!"

The voice of the truck driver echoed through the warehouse, interrupting their conversation and Indie headed his way.

"Yo, can I use your cell? My shit's dead. No car charger," he stated in frustration.

Indie tossed Ethic his phone without a second thought. "I'm going to make sure the truck is straight before he pulls out. Come out when you're done with your call."

Ethic nodded and watched Indie disappear. As soon as he was alone, Ethic rifled through Indie's contacts until he saw her name. He hit the call button slyly as his eyes watched the door. He had to hear from her while he was in town. She was the whole reason why he had come back . . . business was just the excuse he told himself to make it all make sense.

The fact that YaYa hadn't heard from Indie since she had stormed out only added to her fury. Silence felt like indifference and that was worse than the cheating itself. How could he really not care that she had walked out of his life? Wouldn't a man who claimed to love her come after her? She was used to this breathing period. She knew that it was his way of letting her cool down, but it always had the exact opposite effect. While Indie thought she was cooling it, she was really heating up. His absence only gave her room to think. Was he with Parker? Was that bitch now living what was supposed to be her picture-perfect life? Had Indie simply moved her out to move Parker in? Did he love Parker more? All of these questions burned in her mind, making it hard to sleep. It had been two days and nothing. He hadn't rung her line once and after the ultimate act of betrayal he had committed she would have thought he would be beating down her door by now. Indie hadn't even called to check on Skylar, which was completely out of character. Parker's reemergence in his life made YaYa feel like a replacement. All of the time that she had known Indie she had thought she was his once-in-a-lifetime love. That their souls had been assigned to one another long before they had ever met. She had been wrong. Apparently Indie made every woman feel that way, because along came Parker singing the same love song that YaYa had thought originated with her. The reality that Indie had been in love before was crushing. It was a pain that she didn't know existed. It was one thing to have an enemy turn on you. That was to be expected. When the love of your life suddenly showed you shade, however, it was a blow that could be heard around the world. She had shown him vulnerability and he had ultimately betrayed her. She had no respect for a nigga who switched up on her. The way she looked at it, if a nigga could turn on the woman he lay next to every night, there was no limit to the amount of damage he would do to others. Indie had taught her loyalty but when it came down to him showing it to her, he failed. For that, she hated him. She had put her faith in him during times when God should have been her anchor and just like a fake nigga Indie had given up on her when she needed him most. No one, not even her own mother had ever made her feel so small. Love was a motherfucker that's for sure. The tricks it played with the heart were cruel and unusual punishment. As much crying, screaming, brewing she had gone through the past few days she hated that she had ever given up her common sense to love in the first place. How Indie could love her enemy she didn't understand. She did not care what the circumstances were; she would have never chosen anyone over him. *Guess we aren't built the same,* she thought. *That's the problem nowadays. Women know too much about loyalty whereas men know absolutely nothing about it,* she thought. YaYa wanted nothing to do with Indie today, but yesterday she wanted him near. She was sure that tomorrow would bring about a completely different set of confusing emotions. Thus was the life of the broken-hearted. Through her difficulties she was so grateful for her child. Having her was her blessing. She was the most reliable piece of Indie there was and it seemed that Skylar knew that YaYa needed her. She was overly affectionate toward YaYa and her tiny kisses were like little bandages to all of YaYa's emotional wounds. Skylar had no idea the type of strength she was giving to her mom, but YaYa was well aware.

Indie's name lit up her phone and just like that YaYa's heart paced. Everything in her wanted to ignore him, but out of habit she slid the bar across the bottom of the screen to accept the call.

"Hello?" was her greeting.

"Where are you?"

YaYa's mouth fell open in complete surprise. It wasn't Indie's voice that she heard but an unexpected baritone filled her ear.

"I'm at the Trump Towers near Central Park," she whispered.

Click.

She knew that it meant he was on his way and she couldn't wait to see his face again. Ethic was everything right about a man and as much as she wanted to fight the attraction that she felt for him, right now, he was just what she needed.

The faithfulness that had been established to Indie over the years caused a pit of guilt to form in her stomach, but his betrayal reminded her that she had nothing to feel guilty about. She had every right to do whatever the hell she wanted to do. Right?

Ethic hung up the phone and then deleted the most recent call. Indie reentered the room and Ethic passed him the phone. "I'm out of here," he said. "I'll be in touch when that shipment arrives."

"You're leaving already? Kick back, let's celebrate this first run. Have a drink," Indie stated.

Ethic shook his head as thoughts of YaYa filled his mind. "I'm good. There's nothing to celebrate yet. When this thing is moving like a well-oiled machine, then I'll pop a bottle," he said. "I'll be in touch."

He left Indie's office and hopped into his G-Class Mercedes truck, pulling out into full traffic at top speed.

He wasn't sure what it was about YaYa that made him want to get involved. Yes, she was beautiful, but he wasn't a stranger to bad bitches. Her body was amazing, but he had indulged with the supermodel type before. It was something else . . . something interior that intrigued him about YaYa; he just couldn't put his finger on it. He didn't care if she was Indie's girl. *The nigga don't know how to handle that,* Ethic thought. Had he and Indie been friends, Ethic would never approach YaYa, but they weren't. They were brought together on a money plot. Their relationship was straight business so he had no qualms about going after what he wanted. Men like Indie failed to realize that what he had neglected to appreciate was the exact thing that the next man would. While Indie was running off with Parker, Ethic was running toward YaYa.

Ethic arrived at the hotel and left his truck with the valet as he made his way up to YaYa's floor. It was as if an unknown force was pulling him her way because as much as his mind told him to turn around and leave, he kept going forward. He was the metal to her magnet. The moth to her flame. Nothing had felt this familiar since . . . let's just say it had been years since something had felt so innately right. He knocked on her door and she answered it with a smile so bright that it lit up his entire world. He could see her pain, smell it, feel it as it radiated off of her. Her red eyes let him know that she had cried herself to sleep consecutively. Her hair was disheveled and she was wrapped in a silk robe. There was nothing glamorous about her appearance, but he found her imperfectly perfect. He had never seen her so beautiful. Her vulnerability was the most alluring.

"I thought you went back home," she whispered.

"I did. I had to come back, meet with Indie about business," Ethic said.

The sound of his name caused her eyes to water. Here she was, her world was on freeze. She was suffering from heartbreak and Indie had gone on without missing a beat. It was business as usual for him.

"He knows you called me?" she asked.

"He doesn't. I deleted the call," Ethic said.

"Why did you call?" she asked.

"Can I be honest?" he countered.

"Please do," she replied. "I can't handle any more lies from men."

"I haven't stopped thinking about you since the day I met you," Ethic said. He pushed her through the door and stepped over the threshold into her suite. His lips touched hers and she closed her eyes as tears ran down her cheeks. The gloriousness behind their kiss made it feel as if she had taken a breath of fresh air after being emotionally drowned for days. She felt so many things as she felt him untie her silk robe with ease. Guilt, uncertainty, pain all pulsed through her because the hands that were massaging her firm nipples were not Indie's. However, pleasure, infatuation, lust, and the faint trace of love swirled in her heart as Ethic handled her in the way that only a real nigga could. He was everything that Indie was not. While he shared all of the boss-like qualities that Indie possessed, he also had the qualities that Indie lacked. Right now he was rescuing her from a dying love and for that she was so grateful.

She felt Ethic pull back in hesitation.

"Please don't stop," she whispered as she caressed the side of his face and stared him directly in his eyes.

He rested his forehead on hers. "You know once you give me that, I'm going to want to keep it," he said.

She gasped as she felt his thumb massage her clitoris, slowly. "I want you, ma," Ethic whispered. "All of you . . . even your heart."

YaYa pull his face nearer as she initiated his kiss. "That's all I want is to be wanted," she answered. "You can have me."

She felt his need pressing into her stomach as he slid the silk kimono robe off of her shoulders. Her flower was already dripping with her own nectar and like a bee to honey Ethic's attraction grew stronger. He laid her on the bear rug that covered the hardwood floors and spread her legs east and west.

"Wait, wait," she moaned. "You need a condom," she whispered.

Ethic would be the first man that she had slept with in years. She wanted to do this, more than he knew, but they barely knew one another and the foreign nature of their relationship scared her. She trusted him, but she knew that there was still so much to learn. YaYa wasn't young and naïve anymore. She had given herself to a lot of niggas back in the day, without thinking twice. Now she was wiser, older, and had a child to live for.

She had no idea that Ethic found the request incredibly sexy and as a man he always came prepared. He opened his wallet and removed a Magnum, staring her in the eyes as he rolled it snugly over his length. He wasted no time in parting her. She gasped in amazement at his girth as he worked his hips, grinding slowly as she matched his stroke. She rolled over on all fours as she dipped her back low. YaYa wanted him to beat it up. She was in need of a punishment and as he gripped her hips as he entered from behind her mouth fell open. The line between pleasure and pain was so thin that she had to bite her lip to stop herself from calling out his name. He reached around and fondled her clit as she threw it back. She came, within minutes and then collapsed onto her stomach as he lay on top of her, sweeping the baby hairs off the nape of her neck while kissing her gently.

"I've thought about you too," she whispered. She rolled around so that she faced him. "Indie and I are done."

"Are you sure?" he asked.

She nodded. "He let another woman come between us," she said. "There is no coming back from that."

"I don't like to play the sucker, ma. If this is just a rebound thing, something on the side to make you feel better, then lay that out for me now," Ethic said.

"I wish it was that simple," YaYa said. She couldn't stop herself from kissing him. "But I feel something for you. I'm too emotional to fully understand what it is, but I do know that I don't want this feeling or you to go away."

He stood and began to dress. "Where are you going?" she asked, almost panicked. She didn't want her good thing to leave just yet. He was a beautiful distraction from the disaster that had become her life. She silently wondered if her entire relationship with Indie had only occurred so that fate could align her path with Ethic's. YaYa wasn't a fall in love type of girl. She had only done it once, but with Ethic she could see herself going through the inconvenience again. She would have to be careful to always remain the one who loved the least. She had given Indie too much of herself. She would always maintain the upper hand with Ethic, to avoid being hurt again.

"I've got to go. My girls are here with me. They're back at my hotel suite with the nanny," Ethic said.

She was saddened by his sudden departure, but she understood. "When do you leave town?" she asked.

"I don't know just yet," Ethic said as he buttoned his final button on his Prada shirt. "You just gave me a reason to stick around for a while."

She smiled and he bent over to kiss her. "Good," she responded with a smile.

"Good night, beautiful. I'll be in touch."

YaYa stood, unashamed in her nakedness as she walked him to the door. She hated to see him go, but she knew that he would be back. Getting a man had never been an issue for her. Indie must have forgotten how intoxicating her love could truly be. She closed the door behind him and finally exhaled. Ethic's presence tended to make her hold her breath. Her head was spinning and as she headed to her shower she couldn't help but smile at just how quickly the tables had turned. When she passed the mirror she couldn't help but stop and admire her smile. It was the first real sign of happiness that she had expressed in days and it felt good to know that it was possible to feel content without Indie in her life. Ethic didn't know it but his presence gave her hope. It was only because of him that YaYa was sure that she could move on after heartbreak. A split from Indie was not the end of her world, despite the way that it felt at the moment. She was strong. She had endured much more and survived worse; little did she know the worst was yet to come.

Chapter 19

"So now that this thing is officially in your lap, when do you get plugged with the connect?" Trina asked as she sat, breaking down a brick of cocaine. Miesha sat across from her; both wore masks and gloves to protect themselves from the residue and scent of the potent narcotic. They were the only two that Chase would trust with his product. He knew that they would eventually have to expand their circle, but until he could find worthy additions, they all were putting in overtime to make their thing run smoothly. Chase was a jack of all trades. He had access to the finest "fish scale" that money could buy. He was getting bricks in by the boatload and there was no limit. As long as he could flip it then Indie would supply it and Chase wasn't going to miss a single dollar. In addition to moving weight to heavy hitters in other boroughs, he also broke the bricks down and distributed it through Harlem and Brooklyn. With the lack of leadership in the underworlds of those boroughs, Chase couldn't see himself turning a blind eye to the open market. He was even expanding and stepping out of Indie's shoes by moving into DC and Baltimore. The streets were on lock, there was just one problem . . . the Dominicans.

"I don't need to meet the connect. I fucks with Indie. That's enough of a plug for me," Chase stated as he loaded a stack of money in the counting machine. The bills flipped through making music to Chase's ears.

"Getting it from Indie is like having a middle man. You know he putting a tax on it. Why not just ask him to plug you straight with the source?" Trina pushed.

"Because that's greedy, T. You've got to learn about business etiquette. Indie could have easily kept his position in the streets and kept me as a worker. Instead, when he grew he allowed me to grow, so he deserves to eat off the top. Cutting him out ain't loyal. He didn't have to put me on, but he did. You've got to step outside of yourself, Trina. It's not always about cutting people off. You've got to remain true to the niggas that have kept it one hundred with you. Indie and Ya are family. What's up with you lately? All I've been hearing is you talking reckless about this situation lately. What's the beef? You're eating right?"

Miesha was silent as she watched Chase and Trina banter. She had never been the one to intervene in family business, but she too had noticed Trina's disposition when it came to their team.

"Yeah, I'm eating but at what cost?" she asked. "Like I told Miesha, Indie and especially YaYa are all about them . . . so I'm going to be all about me. It was love in the beginning, but I feel like at the end of the day, we are simply pawns. I'm telling you. All three of us are expendable."

"Kill all that noise you talking, Trina. We're good," Chase said as he held up a thick wad of bills, all hundreds. "Are we not good?"

Trina sighed and shook her head as she continued to cut the coke. "Yeah, we good."

Chase knew his sister like the back of his hand but he couldn't understand where this new doubt was coming from. He needed her to get out of her feelings and stay focused. She had been a trooper when Indie was in charge and now that this was Chase's show he needed her now more than ever. Her head wasn't on straight. She was sensing snake in people that he trusted with his life and it made him uncomfortable. She was blood. He needed her on board.

"Let's call it a night. We can wrap this shit up in the morning," Chase declared.

"You don't like what I've got to say about your people so you kicking me out?" Trina asked, seeing through Chase.

"Without 'my people' we would still be back in Houston eating instant noodles and stomping on roaches, T!" Chase reminded her harshly. "Mama didn't give a fuck. The schools didn't. The social workers didn't. Guess who did? Indie. He pulled us out of hell! Or did your red bottoms and thousand-dollar weaves make you forget?"

Trina pulled the mask off her face and removed her gloves as she stood to her feet. "I ain't forget shit," Trina spat. "But I don't owe anybody a lifetime debt. I'm out! Fuck you and this bullshit-ass team," she said. She stormed out of the apartment, leaving Miesha and Chase stunned to silence.

"Fuck is wrong with her? You know what that was all about?" Chase asked as he swiped his neat waves with his hands in frustration. Just when he had come into his own, his own family was adding conflict to the equation. "I don't need that shit right now."

"I don't know. I know that when I did the bid for YaYa, Trina felt a kind of way about it. She didn't think I should do it. I do know that when I got out she was different. I don't think she likes how close YaYa and I have gotten. I think she just feels lost in all of this. Like we are all a family, but she doesn't know her role," Miesha informed.

"Well she better work this shit out real quick," Chase said.

"I can stay and finish up here if you want to go after her," Miesha offered.

Chase shook his head. "Nah, I'm good. Let her clear her head. I'd rather be in good company. She killing my vibe with all that negative shit. Besides I can't leave you in the trap by yourself. I'd have to blow a nigga head off for running up in here on you, ma," he said.

"Aww," she teased jokingly. "I didn't know you cared."

"I care," was his simple reply.

His statement caught her off-guard and she cleared her throat. She didn't know if she was taking his words out of context, but it felt like he was coming at her. *Is he flirting with me?* she asked herself. Chase had known her since she was a young girl and not once had he come at her.

"Since when?" she asked.

Chase looked at her. His eyes shone nothing but truth as he replied, "Since always."

A flutter in her stomach caused her to smile as she realized what this was. He was seeing her for the young woman she had become and not the teenage girl he had met years ago.

"Chase, I . . ."

He stood to his feet and replied, "We ain't got to talk about it. Right now I'm building. I'm in grind mode. When I'm ready for you, you'll know."

She smiled, completely flattered because she knew that he meant every word.

Before she could respond the sound of bullets shattering glass rat-tat-tatted throughout the house.

Chase immediately dove for her, putting his body over hers as he pushed her to the ground. "Stay down," he said. The way the bullets were coming he knew that if he didn't bust back the assailants were going to move in on them. *Fuck it,* he thought as he came up off his waist and began sending hollow points back their way. The gunshots were like tiny bolts of thunder as light emanated from his gun. With every resounding blast Miesha jumped out of her skin. It was clear the way that the living room was getting chopped up that the goons had come to kill. She couldn't die on her knees under a table, not after Chase had revealed he had feelings for her. She hadn't even lived yet, fuck dying. She crawled low across the floor until her back was against the door that the goons were threatening to come through. They were so busy shooting at Chase that they had no clue that she was even inside. She held out her hand to Chase to signal for him to stop shooting.

His ceasefire was all the go-ahead that the goons needed to proceed into the house, but as soon as the first guy stepped over the threshold . . .

Boom!

Miesha stuck her hand out and dropped him at point-blank range. The second shooter began spraying reck-lessly, but Miesha dropped to the floor and aimed at both of his knees.

Boom! Boom!

He fell to the floor, his weapon flying out of his grasp as he grabbed his knees in excruciation.

Chase stood, completely amazed at Miesha's fearless-ness. She was his exact ideal of the type of chick his lady should be. He knew that she had the hustle down and yes, he even knew that she knew how to shoot a gun. He had made sure that she and Trina were both excellent shots in case they needed to protect themselves. He had no clue that her gunplay was so efficient, however. She was nice with the hardware and he found her incredibly sexy in that moment. She hadn't hesitated to put in work. Where most women would have frozen Miesha did what needed to be done. *No wonder YaYa sent her inside to get at Leah,* he thought. Chase ran up on the injured goon, enraged as he pulled the leaking man up by his collar.

"Who sent you?" Chase roared as he delivered a hard blow to the man's face with the butt of his gun.

"Fuck you, you pussy!" the man roared.

"Pussy?" Chase asked with a chuckle as he pulled the man's mask off.

"The Dominicans?" Miesha asked as she stood off to the side a bit shaken.

"Eduardo sent you? You bitch-ass nigga! Huh?" Chase chastised the man as he brought his gun up, only to smash it over his face at full force repeatedly.

The man was a blubbering pulp as he took the beating. Finally, he whimpered, "Please, no more . . . it was *Señor* Eduardo. He sent us. Indie killed his son."

Chase staggered back, covered in the man's blood as he realized what the man had just said. Trina and Miesha had murdered the only son of the Dominican mobster; now Eduardo was out for Indie's blood. He didn't know that Chase had taken over. He put the blame at the top. Chase had just gotten Indie a new beef. Chase extended his arm and . . .

Pop! Pop!

Two bullets to the face and the goon was silenced forever.

"We have to call Indie," Miesha whispered, realizing what this meant. She and Trina had potentially started a war.

"No, we don't. This is my beef. I'll handle it," Chase stated. He looked up at Miesha. Her eyes were wide and fear filled. He walked over to her and pressed her against the wall until she had nowhere to go. They stared at one another with aggression.

"Eduardo tried to rob us. We didn't have a choice," she defended.

"I know that, you know that, but Big Eduardo thinks his son was killed in cold blood and he's blaming Indie. Don't worry. I'll fix it. You trust me?" he asked.

She nodded.

"Then keep this between us. The last thing I need is Indie thinking I can't handle my new position. Go home, clean yourself up. I'll swing by later to check on you, a'ight?" he asked.

She nodded and he leaned in to kiss her lips. Despite the dead bodies around them, sparks flew as she returned his passion. Yep, this was the beginning of a new Bonnie and Clyde. They could both feel something epic growing between them.

"What about the bodies?" she asked.

"I'll clean it up. Go home. Don't tell anybody. Not even Trina," he reiterated. He pecked her lips one last time and then smacked her on her ass in reassurance as she walked out of the house.

"I can really get these? Mama never buys me Jordans!" King exclaimed as he placed his feet inside the pair of $150 kicks.

"Yeah, li'l man, you can get whatever you want," Indie said.

"You're going to spoil him," Parker stated sternly.

"My little nigga got to be fly," Indie replied. "None of this corny shit you got him in."

Parker gave Indie the side eye and he chuckled as he pulled her close, throwing an arm around her shoulder. "No worries, ma, I'm not a knucklehead. I'm buying him all this, but I've also had my accountant set up a savings and college fund for him. He's also been added to my life insurance. I told you, now that I'm around I got you. I've got you both. Now why don't you wander into Neiman's or something while we finish up here." He passed her his black card and she smirked as she shook her head incredulously and walked away.

He watched her go, enjoying the view from behind before turning around to sit next to his son. "You like how those feel, King?" he asked.

"Yeah, these are dope," King replied, excitedly. "Pick out a few more pairs. We'll pick up some clothes next."

"Really?" King asked. It wasn't that he didn't have clothes. Parker made sure that he was well cared for, but the fact that he was going shopping with his dad meant the world to him.

"Yeah, homie, whatever you want," Indie confirmed. As he watched King browse through the store his mind drifted to Skylar. It had been two weeks since he had seen her and he missed the morning kisses that she would deliver each day. He wondered how she was. How was YaYa? They were constantly on his mental.

Life without YaYa was like living without oxygen. It was like everything around him was standing still and Indie ached for her companionship. Although he was going through the motions with Parker, it didn't quite feel the same. The history between them made his presence feel obligatory instead of natural. Parker and King had already established a rhythm, an entire life that didn't include him, so now that he was trying to be around it felt forced. Being the head of YaYa's home was as natural as the air he breathed. He missed her. His core yearned to be near her, but he knew that right now he was the last person that she wanted to see. Indie had never meant to hurt anyone; he was simply in over his head. Before Parker had come back, Indie had never even fathomed the idea of stepping out on YaYa. His love for Parker had been so deep that when she left he had always pondered the what-ifs. Only the love of his life could make him cheat on the love of his life. Most people never found their other half, but here he was burdened with the possibility that two different women could possibly be "the one" for

him. He had fallen in love twice; now he was being forced
to choose between them. Indie wanted to call YaYa. He
wanted to apologize, to explain his predicament. Perhaps
even beg YaYa for her forgiveness, but he did none of
those things. He had rehearsed what he would say to
her in his mind a hundred times, but none of it sounded
right. Instead he gave her space, partly because he knew
that no words would excuse his actions. No "I'm sorry"
would ever erase the pain that he had caused. A woman
scorned never fully healed and he knew that YaYa would
never love him the same again. Even if she accepted
him back into her life, even if she said the words "I love
you," he knew that they it would all be a lie. The wall of
resentment that she would build around her heart would
be impenetrable. They would simply be going through
the motions. So what was the point in calling? It seemed
that he had taken his own options away because the only
one left on the table was Parker and while he did feel
something for her, it was becoming clear that it wasn't the
same as the love he had for Disaya.

The last thing he wanted was to end up alone, however,
Parker had his seed. King was someone he desperately
wanted to know. He owed that little boy the world and had
so much lost time to make up for. He was just so unsure
about making promises to another woman. Parker wanted
a family. She wanted security . . . fidelity, companionship,
and exclusivity. Indie had promised YaYa all those same
things and when he had come up short, it hurt him just as
much as it did her. He didn't want to disappoint Parker,
especially when his heart wasn't 100 percent hers. Indie
was slowly beginning to realize that he had become the
type of man that he never wanted to be. He belonged to the
money and whatever woman fit into his life at the moment
was whom he chose. His actions had forced YaYa out, but
was it now okay to let Parker in? His heart said no, but his

logic told him that he owed Parker after his own mother chased her out of town. He had to see what was in the cards for them.

"That'll be six hundred dollars, sir."

The sound of the cashier's voice snapped him out of his reverie and he paid the balance, grabbed the bags and left, holding King's hand.

As he met up with Parker he decided that if he was going to be with her then the two of them together would need to sit down with Elaine and air out the past. He had already lost YaYa; he refused to push his mother away as well. He would need her to help sort out his mixed emotions and to support whatever decision he made when it came to his life.

This is too soon. Why am I even here? I can't feel what I'm feeling for this man. I don't even know him. I haven't even gotten closure with Indie yet. All of these things ran wild in YaYa's mind as she held Skylar's hand while walking through Central Park. She was meeting Ethic, at his request, but all of her internal warnings were sounding off. She had never been afraid to explore her emotions before, but this affair with Ethic was new territory for her. The fact that he was in business with Indie made her feel like what she was doing was wrong. *This will lead to disaster. Just walk away. Turn around and leave and don't think about him again. This cannot happen.*

She was trying to convince herself to jump out of the fire before she got burnt, but when she saw him, standing so handsome before her, all of her protests were in vain. The single-breasted Margiela coat he wore bossed him out as he stood, oblivious to the fact that she was watching him. His stature, his presence, his aura was strong and she couldn't stop the silly schoolgirl smile that graced her face. He stood watching kids as they ran frantically on the playground.

"Hi," she greeted, when she finally approached.

"Hi," he responded. He looked down at Skylar.

"This is Skylar," she said. She bent down and picked up her daughter, holding her in her arms. "Sky, this is Ethic. This Mommy's friend."

Skylar blushed and held on to her neck tightly. "Can I go play?"

"Sure, baby," YaYa said. "She's shy," she said to Ethic.

"I remember those days," he said. He cupped his hands over his mouth and shouted, "Bella!"

A beautiful young girl came running over to him. "Yes, Daddy?" she said.

"Come here, I want you to meet a special friend of mine. This is YaYa. YaYa, this is my daughter Bella," he introduced.

YaYa was taken aback. She hadn't expected this, but it was a pleasant surprise. "Nice to meet you, Bella. This is my daughter Sky."

"Nice to meet you too, ma'am," she replied.

YaYa chuckled. "Please just call me YaYa," she responded.

Ethic pulled a twenty dollar bill out of his wallet and handed it to Bella. "Why don't you take Skylar to that ice cream truck and then show her around the playground, baby girl. Be careful. Keep a close eye out. She's much younger than you."

"Okay," Bella agreed. She held out her arms and to YaYa's surprise Skylar went to her without hesitation.

"How old is she?" YaYa asked.

"A very mature twelve," he replied.

"She's gorgeous," YaYa complimented.

"She gets it from her mother," Ethic replied, humbly.

"Raven, right?" YaYa asked.

Ethic shook his head. "No. Bella's mother was before Raven. She died. My son Ezra," he said as he pointed to the slide where his five-year-old played rambunctiously. "That's him. He's the gift that Raven gave me. Their nanny brought them to New York with me, seeing as how I don't know how long I'm going to stay. I sent for them last night."

"Wow, so you're a family man and a gangster all at the same time," she said as she nudged him jokingly.

"They come first," he said. "The nanny, Ms. Gwen, she helps tremendously, but other than that I'm a single father. I have a teenager, she's seventeen. She's Raven's sister. I adopted her after Raven died. She's back in Flint, however. She's my challenge."

"I don't know what to say," YaYa replied honestly. "Your life seems so . . ." She paused.

"Complicated?" he asked.

"Yeah, a little," she admitted.

"Did the kids scare you off?" he asked.

"Not even a little," she replied.

It was so crazy to her how Ethic seemed to take away all the bad whenever she was in his presence. Her entire life hung in the balance at the moment. Just this morning she had cried her eyes out while staring at her own reflection. Thoughts of losing Indie and of what he might be doing with the next woman consumed her at all other times, except now, in this moment with Ethic, she had no worries. Ethic was like convenient amnesia. He made her entire body tingle and soothed her soul to the point of contentment.

"Good," he said with a warm smile. They faced the playground as they stood side by side. "I understand your situation, ma, but I also understand my limitations. I'm not a secret keeping type of nigga. When I want to see your face, I want the freedom to come through. When I want to hear your voice, I want to be able to call. I don't want to meet in hotel rooms or seedy restaurants. When I want to feel your body under mine, I want to be able to have you. You can't give me that, can you?"

YaYa's heart ached because she wanted to be able to tell him that she could. She wanted to throw caution to the wind and be his woman . . . only his woman, but wasn't she still considered Indie's woman? Not even she knew where she stood in her own relationship and she didn't want to play games with a man like Ethic. He wouldn't tolerate them and she knew that he was undeserving of her indecision.

"I don't know," she answered honestly. "I want to be able to give you all of those things. The way my body craves you is ridiculous. Like right now, I feel a pulse inside of me that I've never felt before. It makes me want to touch it. It makes me want to touch you, to love you. To just say fuck everybody who would want me without you. You make me feel different than any man ever has."

He turned toward her. "I'm feeling you, YaYa, some people might even say I'm loving everything about you, but you're not ready."

"It doesn't help that you're in business with Indie," she stated.

"Fuck business with Indie, ma. I'm good. My bank was large before I entered into business with him. I'm willing to cut that if necessary. You just have to tell me I'm not doing it all for nothing. I can't be in it dolo. If your heart is with that man then walk away," he said. "You can leave right now and I'll respect it but if you stay, be sure that this is what you want."

She held her head down as tears came to her eyes. She folded her hands across her chest and replied, "I'm not sure of anything right now. I do know the only time I'm not sad is when I'm with you."

"I'm not putting pressure on you, YaYa. When you figure it out, you let me know. Until then maybe you just need to focus on you, ma. It flatters me that I make you smile. I love that because that smile definitely does something to me," he said as he gave her a charming grin of his own and placed a hand over his heart as if he had been struck by Cupid's bow. "But your happiness should depend on you, not me, or any other man. You understand?"

Lawd, why is this man so damn fine? she asked herself, completely smitten by Ethic. His words of wisdom were received with nothing but respect because she knew that he was right.

She nodded and leaned against him as she looped her hand through his arm. "You're a good man, Ethic."

"Not to everyone. There are a lot of people out there that would tell a different story." He smirked.

"I could never believe that," she said. As they stood in silence, watching their children play, for a brief moment it felt like a family. YaYa could be this man's wife and these could be their children in some other life. Sadly, in this reality she was just a lonely girl in an even lonelier world. She pulled back and said, "We're going to go okay?"

"I think that's probably best," he replied. He leaned over and planted the softest kiss on her forehead. It was more intimate than any kiss that had ever been placed on her lips. "See you later, beautiful."

She smiled as she walked over to Skylar and scooped her in her arms before departing. She hoped that when she turned back, Ethic would still be watching her. As she glanced subtly she smiled because he was eyeing her every move. *I ain't lost it,* she thought in amusement as she disappeared out of his sight.

Chapter 20

"Why are we here? You know how Elaine feels about me," Parker protested as a knot formed in her stomach.

"You're going to be around," Indie said. "We have to work this out. My mom is important to me and so are you. I need the two of you to respect one another. I also know that my father will want to meet his grandson."

Indie climbed out of the car and Parker groaned reluctantly as she followed suit. King hopped out the back, his face buried in his handheld PlayStation as the threesome walked to the front door.

Indie knocked, deciding not the use his key. He wanted Elaine to answer the door and welcome Parker into her home. The smell of her Southern cooking permeated through the door and Parker said, "She's probably poisoning my plate as we speak," Parker cracked before laughing playfully.

Indie couldn't help but smirk as his mom opened the door.

"Hey, ma," he greeted.

"Hey, baby," she said. He kissed her cheek and stepped inside. Parker placed her hand on King's back and guided him inside.

"Hi, Elaine," Parker said, forcing politeness.

"Parker," Elaine responded, equally forced.

"Mama," Indie stated sternly. Elaine looked down at the little boy in front of her and she instantly warmed to him. She looked at Parker in shock. "This is Indie's boy?" she asked.

"Of course it is," Parker shot back. Elaine looked skeptically at Parker. She had so much to say but held her tongue. Parker bent down to his speak to her son. "King, this is your grandmother, Elaine," she said as she gave his arm a squeeze reassuringly. She stood and presented her son to Elaine.

"Hi, King. It's very nice to meet you," Elaine spoke as she looked down at him. He was so familiar to her, but it wasn't Indie who he reminded her of.

"Where's Pop?" Indie asked.

"You know where he is . . . in that den in front of the TV. The Lions are playing. Grab a seat. Parker can help me set the table," Elaine insisted.

Parker looked skeptically at Indie who gave her a wink of reassurance. Parker, however, felt like she was being fed to the wolves.

"Come on, King. You can watch the game with the boys, homie," Indie said as he guided his son with pride out of the room.

Elaine led the way into the kitchen and over to her cabinets. She pulled out five place settings and handed them to Parker.

"So this is awkward," Parker stated.

Elaine looked at her as if she was made of plastic. She had always had the gift of spotting fake from a mile away. She wasn't buying Parker's act. "Why are you here, Parker? That boy had a family . . . a good girl that he loved."

"He loves me. He has me now and King," Parker responded as she set the table.

"Hmm, hmm. He does. He always did. You always had your fingernails stuck in his back. You were a charmer but if my memory serves me right, he wasn't the only one of my sons you kept time with," she said.

Parker's eyes widened. "Elaine, please," she whispered as she looked to make sure that Indie wasn't coming.

"King needs a father," Parker stated.

"You need to tell Indie the truth. If you don't, I will," Elaine threatened.

"Oh my God," Parker moaned as she spread her arms out over the hood of the '84 classic red Cutlass Supreme. Nanzi slid in and out of her wetness, showing her no mercy as he explored the depths of her cave. He was a beast in the bed and he commanded her body with every stroke, blowing her young mind. She didn't know how she had let this happen. How she had gone from a virgin to having sex with Indie and his brother Nanzi she didn't know. It just happened. She was in love with Indie. He was her future, her motivation, her pride but Nanzi was her present. Their attraction was purely sexual. He ravaged her and being a few years older than Indie, he knew how to make her body cream in ways that Indie had yet to discover.

Her guilt ate away at her whenever she was with Indie, but as soon as Nanzi was in her presence again she always felt the familiar pulse of wanting beating between her thighs. It had all started the day that Nanzi's hands had slipped beneath her bikini bottoms while she was sitting in a hot tub with him and Indie. Nanzi's fingers had brought her to orgasm beneath the bubbles without anyone even noticing. Their affair only gained steam from there. Now here she was bent over his car in the scorching garage, taking all eight inches of him and loving it. Her betrayal was the ultimate disrespect but she just couldn't help herself. Nanzi was bad, dangerous, and sometimes she even feared him but all of those things made him sexually irresistible. She knew it was wrong and each time she kept telling herself she was going to stop but every time he saw her, it was like he owned her. One look and she knew that they were fucking. She had gotten caught up between brothers.

She loved Indie, heart and soul, but her body belonged to Nanzi. There was just something about the wild young boy that drove her mad. She didn't know if his was his tattooed body, his experienced manhood, or his skillful tongue but Parker could never break his hold over her.

Her legs quivered as he stroked her into an orgasm and as she called out his name the garage door lifted. They scrambled frantically trying to adjust their clothing but Elaine's eyes witnessed their betrayal before they were able to cover their tracks.

"Nanzi, get your ass in the fucking house," she said. She had such a coldness to his tone that he knew not to protest. He simply buttoned his jeans and walked away, leaving Parker to face his mother.

"Get out of my house, little girl," Elaine spat while looking at her in disgust.

Parker rushed out of the garage with her head hung in shame but Elaine's voice halted her. "And stay away from my son," she warned. "Both of them."

Parker remembered that day like it was yesterday and shame filled her all over again. She had tried to stay away from Indie, but he loved her. Nothing, not even a breakup could keep him away from her. They continued to see each other against Elaine's wishes and Elaine never told what she had seen that day. It wasn't long before Nanzi's jealousy reared its ugly head however. Despite Parker's beliefs, Nanzi's attraction to her was much more than physical. He was feeling her and secretly wished that Indie and Parker would grow apart. It wasn't until she ended up pregnant did things hit the fan. She hadn't even known, but Elaine did. She noticed all of the signs. Her days of tricking under Buchanan Slim had allowed her to be able to sniff a pregnant bitch out with ease. So when Parker showed up at her house one day, bosom full, face radiant, but looking as if something was draining the life out of her, Elaine already knew. It was then that she made the choice that Parker wasn't going to trap either of her sons. She didn't know which one of them the baby belonged to, but she knew that if Indie found out about Nanzi and Parker that her sons would be adversaries forever. That was the reason she paid Parker $20,000 to get an abortion and leave town. She wasn't trying to sabotage her son, but to save him from a heartbreak that would alter his ability to love.

"I was young. Nanzi is dead," Parker whispered as she placed both hands on the table as she spoke to Elaine. "Why would you throw dirt on his name now? Just let us be a family."

Elaine scoffed and shook her head. "Like I said, Indie has a family and I'm not going to let him play daddy to a child that might not be his. You tell him."

"Tell me what?" Indie asked as he walked into the kitchen with a smile. He motioned toward the den. "King loves his grandfather already. Pops is talking about taking him fishing."

"That's good, baby. I'm going to go in there to spend some time with the newest grandbaby. I believe Parker has something she needs to say to you," Elaine pushed.

Indie's smile faded as he turned to Parker. He could sense her nervousness as she twisted her fingers and sighed deeply.

He walked over to her and rubbed her shoulders supportively. "What's wrong, shorty? Moms got you spooked. Don't worry, she'll warm up to you—"

"Indie, I didn't tell you the full story of why your mom paid me to leave town," she started. Tears clouded her vision because she was well aware that she was about to break Indie's heart. She had just gotten him back. He was perfect for her and she feared that once she delivered this blow he would never forgive her.

"You can tell me anything, you know that," he coached, supportively. His affection only weighed her heart down with guilt even more.

"Indie, King might not be your son," Parker whispered, her voice breaking as she delivered the news.

Indie immediately let her go and took a step back from her. Images of YaYa flashed in his mind. He had left her. He had abandoned her for Parker . . . for King. He hadn't seen Skylar in weeks because he was trying to make up for lost time with his son. Now Parker was telling him this? "You told me he was mine," Indie stated, locking his jaw and keeping his voice low so that King wouldn't overhear.

"I know," she said.

"He looks like me. My eyes, my nose . . ."

"Please let me finish," she whimpered, knowing that she hadn't delivered the heaviest blow just yet.

"Your mom paid me to get the abortion and leave town because she knew about the affair I was having with your brother. I was sleeping with Nanzi and when I got pregnant I didn't know whose baby it was."

Utter devastation took over Indie's face as he balled his fists and placed them on the sides of his head in angst. He paced and then suddenly lunged at her, his temper flaring. He pinned her against the wall and she closed her eyes simply because she didn't want to see that pain that was reflecting in his.

"He's Nanzi's son?" Indie asked. "You broke up my wedding to make me play daddy to a child that isn't mine!"

"I don't know!" she hollered. "I was hoping he was yours," she whispered lowering her tone.

"How long were you sleeping with my brother?" he asked. He felt so much anger. Nanzi and Indie had been thick as thieves, closer than close. He would have never thought the two people who had been closest to him would have cut him so deeply.

She stammered, not wanting to answer his question. "Once? Twice?"

"We were together for a while, Indie," Parker stated.

He squeezed the bridge of his nose and closed his eyes in distress. "Just leave, Parker."

"Indie, this doesn't mean that we still can't do this . . . together," she pleaded. "I do and always have loved you."

"King will be taken care of regardless. If he isn't my son, that means he is my nephew. This family will still support him, but you and I, we're done, shorty," he said. He stormed out of the house, rushing to his car as he realized the detrimental mistake he had made. He had to get to YaYa. In his mind he already knew that it was too late.

YaYa paced back and forth in her suite as her mind spun. She had tried to walk away from Ethic in the park, but as soon as she returned she found herself missing him. Always a phone call away, she requested his presence and he was on his way. Dressed in a La Perla silk robe and red bottom heels, she couldn't wait for him to arrive. Skylar was asleep in the second bedroom so their night should be undisturbed. She was no longer ashamed of her affections for him. After seeing him with his children in the park, she realized that she loved every single thing about that man. She was falling fast and although it scared her, she loved the rush.

Knock! Knock!

She went to the door and opened it without looking but the face she stared into was completely unexpected.

"I need to talk to you, YaYa," Indie said, pain and confusion and regret written all over his face.

YaYa's mouth fell open, taken aback. "How did you know where to find me?" she asked.

"You're my girl, ma. I know you like the back of my hand. This is your favorite suite at your favorite hotel. It wasn't that hard to figure out," he said. "Let me in, ma. I fucked up. I need to talk to you."

"You need to leave," YaYa said as hot tears immediately burned her eyes. How dare the fuck he? Who did he think he was? She hadn't heard from Indie since the night he admitted to sleeping with Parker. He hadn't been concerned about how she was. He hadn't called to check on their child, but he had the nerve to just show up demanding to talk.

"Ya, please. I know I fucked up. I'm so sorry, ma. I love you. I need you, YaYa. Just hear me out," he reasoned.

Panic spread across YaYa's face when she saw Ethic appear over Indie's shoulder. She felt like she was busted, despite the fact that she was doing nothing wrong.

"Ethic," she greeted. Her stomach went hollow as a sick feeling overwhelmed her. *Oh shit,* she thought.

Indie turned around in surprise and his features instantly turned deadly.

"Fuck you doing here?" Indie asked, suddenly obsessed with a jealousy he had never felt. Not even when Parker had revealed that she had sexed his brother did he feel this type of jealousy. His blood boiled as he saw the smile that appeared in YaYa's eyes. Her entire face lit up at Ethic's presence. He could tell she was trying to hide it on his behalf but he knew her too well. She was infatuated.

"I'm here because she asked me to come," Ethic replied as he moved into the suite.

Indie saw red. "Bitch, you fucking my nigga?" He grabbed YaYa by her chin tightly but Ethic grabbed Indie's arm.

"That's not happening tonight, fam, so dead that shit before you catch a problem," Ethic said as he moved his jacket to the side to reveal the burner that sat on his waist.

Indie's fury pumped through his veins making him fearless. "I ain't afraid of gunplay, homeboy, believe that. This is my bitch. You don't have anything to do with how I handle mine."

"Was your bitch," Ethic corrected. "And I have everything to do with it. What happened to that pretty little thing . . ." Ethic snapped his fingers as if he couldn't recall the name. "Parker?"

Indie came up off his hip with his own pistol, but Ethic simultaneously pulled his as well. Having a hot head wasn't even in his nature, but the thought of Ethic with YaYa hurt his soul. He now understood the resentment that YaYa had for him. Knowing that someone else now claimed what was once yours burned like nothing he had ever felt before. There they stood, toe to toe. Boss to boss. Ego to ego, both unflinching. Neither of them had ever pulled their gun without using it. They weren't for show and both understood the rules of the game. Now that they had drawn on one another, one of them had to be Picasso.

"Indie!" YaYa shouted. She stood in the middle, conflicted. Between the man that she loved and one that she was surely falling in love with. "Ethic, please!"

They were so much alike in so many ways, but in the areas that Indie lacked, Ethic was . . . he was perfect. He was loyal and most of all he had been hurt before so he wasn't in the business of dishing out heartbreak.

"Skylar is in the other room!" YaYa stated firmly. She went into the drawer that sat by entryway and pulled out a gun of her own. Both men looked at her in shock. She hadn't lost her gangster. She had simply stifled it because she was trying to live a normal life. She had wanted to be a normal wife for Indie, but stupid she was not. She stayed strapped and the men in her life had lost their minds. If she didn't do something they would gun each other down just to prove which one had the bigger gun.

"My daughter is in the other room," she repeated sternly. "Put your fucking guns up now."

Indie was biting his inner jaw so hard that it had begun to bleed. He could taste the blood as he stared Ethic down. Neither of them flinched. "Indie! Ethic!"

Both men reluctantly lowered their weapons and Indie moved toward the back of the suite. "What are you doing?" YaYa asked.

"You got this nigga up in here while my daughter is here. Fuck that. She's coming home with me," Indie said. "You're fucking him? You fucking him and I do business with him?"

Indie was out of his mind with jealousy and sick to his stomach.

YaYa folded her arms across her chest and watched as he took Skylar out of her bed. She knew that Skylar was fine with her father so she didn't protest. She had planned to tell him about Ethic once she had figured it out herself. She knew how he felt and Skylar would be the best medicine for his shattered heart.

He stormed passed her and stopped when he got in front of Ethic. "I'ma see you," he threatened.

"Likewise," Ethic answered.

He walked out and YaYa let her weight fall to the plush sofa in defeat.

Ethic slowly made his way over to her and sat beside her. He pulled her into his arms. "That's not how I wanted him to find out," she whispered. "This is so messy."

"Do you want me to leave?" Ethic asked.

She looked at him. If she was going to cut him loose, now would be the time to do it. As much as her mind said, *tell him to go,* her heart wanted him to stay. She shook her head. "No. I don't want you to ever go anywhere. I think I feel something for you, Ethic. I don't want to call it love because we really barely know one another, but whatever this is . . . it's strong."

He kissed her lips and she got sucked into his aura effortlessly. It was the sweetest kiss and the gentlest touch that she had ever felt. Any guilt that she felt about Indie finding out instantly melted at Ethic's touch.

"Tell me this, gangster," Ethic commented with a smile. "Where did you learn to handle a gun like that?" he asked.

YaYa thought back to all of her younger years. She had done and seen it all. From tricking niggas, to hustling, to running her own empire. There was no simple answer to his question and she realized how much about her that he did not know. "Let's just say that I'm not a stranger to the life that you and Indie are a part of. I've played my role in it over the years." She cleared her throat and changed the subject.

"I'm sorry about messing up the money between you and Indie," she whispered.

He scoffed. "I'm good, ma. I have enough money. Some things are worth more," he said. She placed her hands on the sides of his face and planted soft kisses all over it while looking him in the eyes.

"I think I love you, boy," she whispered. She hadn't even meant to say it. Actually she had spoken her private thoughts, but it was too late to chase the words down. Once they were spoken the universe owned them.

He looked at her, face so serious as he replied, "I've got to teach you to love you, ma, before you can love me. Because your love for me feels amazing. I want you to know what self-love feels like. The love you give is a gift." Lawd! This man's wordplay made her putty in his hands. As his lips covered hers, YaYa felt nothing but bliss and she couldn't wait for the night to come. Karma's a bitch and Indie had just become acquainted with her wrath. He had left YaYa room to explore something new and unfortunately for him, she liked what she had discovered. Ethic was perfect for her in every way and although she felt badly for Indie's pain, she hadn't forgotten his betrayal. He deserved whatever pain he felt.

Chapter 21

"If the Dominicans want to think Indie was responsible for little Eddie's death than let them. I'm not putting myself on the line against the fucking Dominican mafia," Trina stated in protest as she watched Miesha and Chase load up. They literally looked like they were going to war. Bullet proofs, handguns in holsters, Miesha even had a beam rifle. *These two are out of control,* Trina thought.

"Nah, I've got to fix the mess that you helped make. So strap up or shut the fuck up, sis. Your choice," Chase stated.

"I'm not riding out for Indie or YaYa. I'm good," Trina replied with her arms folded.

Chase shook his head and replied, "You've got a lot to learn about loyalty, little sister."

He looked at Miesha. "You ready, baby girl?"

"I'm with you," she promised.

"Let's go pay Eduardo a visit then," Chase responded.

Trina watched as they walked out of the trap house and shook her head in disgrace. She was done following and riding for mu'fuckas who wouldn't do the same for her. In fact this entire New York scene was played to her. It was time to go back home but she had no intentions on leaving empty-handed.

She walked to the living room and peeked out of the window to ensure that Chase and Miesha had pulled off. Once the coast was clear she rushed to the bedroom, heading straight for the safe. She was the only other person besides Chase who knew the combination so she knew that once she hit her lick he would know it was her. She thought about making it look like a robbery, but fuck it. She had put in her dues, now she was going to take what she felt she was owed. She could start her own shit back home in Houston. She didn't need Indie or YaYa's reputation behind her. She had put in enough work over the years that she could unload product with ease. She took twenty bricks out of the safe and placed them in a black duffel. She second-guessed herself for one second before she walked out of the door, but when she remembered how Miesha had rotted in jail for YaYa, she shook all doubt. She wasn't going to end up a casualty to the game especially not trying to prove herself to Indie or YaYa. She felt that they were foul for putting Miesha in that predicament and before they would test her loyalty she was going to be out. She looked back one last time before she stepped over the threshold. It was time for her to go into business for herself. Fuck a Prada Plan, she was about to become the protégé and show YaYa how a chick was really supposed to get this money.

Chase walked into the bar in Spanish Harlem and immediately stuck out like sore thumb. He was the only black face in the establishment and all eyes were immediately on him. It was a hole in the wall, pool hall type spot where the retirees and OGs of the neighborhood went to kick the shit. It was also where Eduardo and a few of his buddies frequented. Chase went to the bar and sat for ten minutes before the bartender reluctantly serviced him.

"Long way from home huh, kid?" the old man said.

"Nah, I'm right where I'm supposed to be. I'm looking for Eduardo," Chase stated.

The bartender's eyes cut across the room and before Chase knew it he had ten guns aimed at him. It seemed as if every patron there was on Eduardo's protection payroll.

"If I don't walk out of this bar in five minutes flat, Eduardo's brains are going to be on the floor," Chase threatened.

A hearty chuckle came from the back of the bar and Eduardo himself emerged through his men. He was low-key in slacks and a nice designer shirt. His shoes shined like new money, matching the sheen of his dark hair.

"Look at your chest," Chase stated.

Suddenly a red beam appeared in the center of his chest. Chase smirked a bit at Miesha's efficiency. She was right on time. He would never put her in this much danger so she was safely perched on the rooftop across the street, looking through the scope of her gun and aiming it directly at Eduardo.

"You want to tell your men to lower their weapons so we can talk?" Chase asked.

Eduardo, not fond of the fact that someone else had the upper hand on him, huffed and then signaled for his men to stand down.

"You're Indie's shooter. The kid that's under him." Eduardo stated. "You have a lot of balls coming in here after Indie had my boy killed."

"That wasn't Indie. That is why I am here, to clear up the confusion and make amends. Indie is no longer in this business. He handed it over to me. During this transition, your son attempted to rob two of my workers. They were only defending themselves when they killed your son and your two men. We intended to do square business. I give you my apologies that things got so out of hand and I offer you this." Chase paused and put a briefcase full of money on the table. It was $100,000 of his own money. Eduardo looked at Chase skeptically and thumbed through the cash before handing it off to one of his goons.

"Apology not accepted and you . . . you're a kid. You can't be a day over twenty-three. I deal with Indie and I'm holding him personally responsible for my Eduardo's demise. An eye for an eye. That's what I live by. Now get out of here before I have my men rip you to pieces," Eduardo spat harshly.

Chase held his tongue and stood up from the table. He knew that he had to get his numbers up because Eduardo was clearly about to wage a war. He had to warn Indie that they had just made a new enemy.

"Good morning, beautiful," Ethic said as YaYa rustled in his arms. It was the first time they had stayed the night together and every minute of it had been magical. Ethic was like a cure for everything bad. If she could bottle up the feeling he gave her and place it for sale, she would be rich. He had the power to heal broken hearts.

"Good morning," she said as he kissed her nose.

"I have something for you," he said as he leaned over and pulled a silver key out of the nightstand drawer. He opened her hand and placed it in her palm.

"What's this?" she asked, confused.

"It's a key to your own place. I don't like the fact that you're living out of a hotel suite with your daughter. You don't seem to want to go back home . . ."

"I can't," she said. "Too many memories are there."

"Well you can make new memories in your new place and hopefully over time, you can include me and my family in your life," he whispered.

She was speechless because Ethic was all man. He took care of her. He catered to her and he wasn't ashamed or reluctant to express how much she meant to him. There relationship was blossoming at an alarming speed, but she had to admit that she was enjoying the ride.

"Will you accept it?" he asked.

She nodded and rolled on top of him to show him just how much she appreciated him.

YaYa thanked Ethic in every single way. It took everything in her to let him leave, but she understood that he wanted to make it back to his own hotel before his children awoke.

"Call me and let me know what you think about the condo. I have some things coming for you so be expecting deliveries all day," he said.

"I'm sure I'll love it," she responded as she kissed him good-bye.

She was showered and out the door in no time as excitement filled her. It wasn't the first time a man had purchased her a piece of real estate, but this one symbolized so much. It symbolized her freedom.

She located the address in the SoHo neighborhood of Manhattan and quickly realized that Ethic had spared no expense. This was prime real estate and it made her wonder how loaded Ethic truly was. He was working with more than old safe money in order to purchase a woman he barely knew a gift this extravagant. She greeted the doorman with a nod as she entered the building.

When she finally found the home that was hers, the views swept her away. The space wasn't great, but that was to be expected in New York City, but it was the perfect size for her and Skylar. "I can't believe he did this," she whispered. It was like stepping into a fairytale, but as she stood there she couldn't help but think of Indie. She was sure that he was hurt, but not more so than she had been when Parker ruined their lives. *Why the hell did he come to see me yesterday anyway? What happened to him and Parker? The grass isn't always greener, asshole,* she thought, but as bitter as her thoughts were she knew that she needed closure. If she had truly moved on, she wouldn't feel so much resentment toward Indie. She was letting him live rent free in her head and as long as she harbored hurt over what he did, she would never truly be free. YaYa picked up her phone and dialed Indie's number. When he answered he didn't speak, he just let silence fill the line. Seconds past before his hurt tone came through.

"You're fucking him?" he asked.

"It wasn't something I planned or did to get back at you. It just happened," she answered. "You left me for Parker. You let her embarrass me when she broke up our wedding. I was hurt and Ethic makes me not hurt," she admitted.

She heard him trying to contain his emotions as he choked out, "You know I never meant for any of this to happen. I've loved you since the day I met you."

"You didn't love me enough to walk away from her though," YaYa replied.

"She was a mistake. The things she used to pull me away from you, it was a lie and I know I fucked up, ma, but I need you," Indie admitted.

"I don't think you do, Indie. You just don't want to see me with the next man," YaYa responded.

Ding Dong!

YaYa frowned as she kept the phone pressed to her ear while walking to the door. "Love doesn't hurt, Indie."

"You're wrong, ma. Love does hurt. It grows and it changes and during those times there are growing pains, but it also endures everything. It overcomes and conquers the challenges. Love isn't perfect but it's ours and it's worth it, YaYa. Come back to me."

Tears accumulated in her eyes as she pulled open the door to find two deliverymen, carrying a big box.

She waved them in and turned her back to finish her call. "Indie . . ." Before she could get the rest of her sentence out of her mouth she was grabbed from behind. "Aghh!" She only got off one scream before a chloroform rag was placed over her face and she was folded into the empty box that the men had carried inside. They hoisted the box up on the dolly and walked out of her apartment calmly. No one would ever suspect that she was kidnapped inside.

Chapter 22

"Disaya!" Indie screamed into the phone. When he heard the sound of the ring tone in his ear he immediately knew that something was wrong. He dialed her right back, only to receive her voicemail. It wasn't until his phone vibrated in his hand and he received an incoming text did he discover just how drastic the situation was.

A picture of YaYa, tied, mouth bound with duct tape, and hanging in the back of a utility van like a piece of meat, appeared before his eyes. His heart exploded as anger pulsed through him. This attack of terror against his family was completely unexpected. He wrecked his brain trying to think of the last beef he had been involved in. He had been very political about the moves he made since becoming involved with Vartex. Indie had made sure to make a clean break from the coke game.

This has to be a beef that bitch nigga Ethic is involved in.

He immediately copied the picture of YaYa and sent it to Ethic. Within seconds Ethic rang his line.

"Have you lost your fucking mind?" Ethic asked. The amount of rage that he expressed over YaYa only infuriated Indie. "Where is she?"

"You tell me. I don't have no open beef in the streets, my nigga, so this is behind you. She is your bitch right?" Indie asked. "When she was with me, she was protected."

"Meet me in the city," Ethic stated as he now began to worry what ghosts from his past had come back to haunt

YaYa. He thought of the body he had caught when he first came to New York City. Had killing Mizan somehow caught up to him? Was YaYa's kidnapping connected to that? Ethic gave Indie the address to the new place that he had just purchased for YaYa. They both hung up the phone. They were rivals, but their love and worry over the same woman bought them together.

Indie picked up Skylar and was about to dial Elaine when he noticed Chase and Miesha pulling into his driveway. He hung up the phone. *My li'l homie always on time,* he thought as he rushed out of the house with his daughter in his arms.

"Miesha, I need you to watch Skylar for me. You got me?" he asked.

"Sure of course," she said as she took the little girl from his arms, no questions asked. She walked into the house as Indie turned to Chase.

"I need to talk to you, big homie," Chase started.

"Nah, Chase I need you to hear me. Somebody grabbed YaYa up off the street. They got her tied up somewhere. This is personal, fam. No note, no ransom, or nothing. They just sent me this," Indie said as he passed Chase his phone with the text message showing YaYa's picture on the screen.

Chase swiped his face in horror because he knew exactly why this had happened. He couldn't help but feel like this was his fault. If he had accepted his fuck-ups as a leader earlier, than perhaps Indie could have stepped in to deescalate the situation before this had ever occurred.

"I know why this happened," Chase said. "Eduardo tried to rob Trina and Miesha during their last exchange. They shot him and two of his goons. Big Eduardo vowed revenge. I thought I could handle it."

Indie pinched the bridge of his nose as his jaw clenched. "Let's go," he said as he hopped in the passenger side of

Chase's car. He was headed to the city to get Ethic. He didn't want to, but they were about to go up against the Dominican mob. Eduardo would have numbers behind him; Indie would need every shooter he had.

"Where's Trina?" he asked.

Chase picked up the phone to dial her line only to be sent to voicemail. He shook his head. "No answer but I got the choppers in the trunk. Wherever they're holding Ya, we're going to get her back."

"We better or I'm going to paint Spanish Harlem red and I ain't talking brush strokes," Indie threatened.

"Do you know why you are here, YaYa?" Eduardo asked as he circled her. Her hands were bound by rope and he had her hoisted up on a meat hook, stripped naked, in a freezer as he stood looking at her like a predator.

She shivered uncontrollably. She was afraid to cry because she didn't want her tears to freeze on her face. Her taped mouth didn't allow her to answer his question.

"I brought you here because you are the closest person to Indie's heart. His people took the closest thing to my heart. My son is maggot food because of him and it's only right that I return the favor," he said.

YaYa closed her eyes. She knew Eduardo. When she was running things they had done good business. She never thought that she would end up a victim of his maniacal ways. She had heard stories about this very freezer and the butcher's tools that sat on the floor beneath her feet only proved his intentions for her.

She watched in horror as he grabbed a meat saw and turned it on. The sound as it spun wrecked havoc on her nerves as her entire body cringed. The hairs on the back of her neck stood up.

"First, I'm going to saw off every fucking finger, then I'm going to peel your skin off the bone," he said, while smiling wickedly, revealing his decaying teeth.

"Hmmmmm!" She screamed through the tape, but she knew that no one would hear her. She was in the basement below the bar. It had been soundproofed for just this purpose. It was Eduardo's torture chamber and YaYa was his victim. She closed her eyes and did the only thing she could think to do: she took herself on a mental hiatus. She had to think of something happy. Something she loved in order to disconnect from what was about to occur. Her daughter's eyes flashed through her mind and then to her own surprise Indie's face appeared. She hadn't even realized it until she was in crisis, but he represented love and peace for her. Too bad she wasn't going to get a chance to see him one last time before she paid the ultimate price for his sins.

Indie, Chase, and Ethic walked into the bar, semi-automatics loaded and aimed.

Rat-Tat-Tat-Tat-Tat!

They were unapologetic about letting their bullets flow, as they sprayed the establishment. They didn't give a damn if they were hitting innocent patrons or not. There were casualties in war . . . fuck it. Ethic and Indie covered Chase as he stopped shooting. He pulled the hand grenade out of his pocket at held it above his head as the bullets finally stopped.

"Listen up. We're here for Eduardo. Anybody move and my man is pulling the clip out of that grenade he's holding," Indie shouted. There weren't many men left standing after their assault. Bodies lay sprawled on the floor and the walls looked like Swiss cheese, but neither Indie nor Ethic cared.

The bartender held his hands up and came from around the bar. "This isn't our fight. Eduardo is in the basement. None of these men work for Eduardo. Let my customers go and you handle your business," the old man said.

Ethic stepped up and removed his 9 mm.

Boom!

The old man fell dead at his feet, startling the other goons in the bar. "Any more suggestions?" he asked. "Let us be clear. You work for Eduardo but you don't have to die for him. Throw your heaters in the middle of the floor and then line up against that back wall."

The six men who were left standing did as they were told and then lined up, hoping that their submission would keep them alive. Indie, Ethic, and Chase followed no rules of engagements when it came to this, however. Getting YaYa out safely meant that everyone involved would pay a price. They didn't know what roles these men had in her abduction but they would serve as an example to the hood that Disaya Morgan was not to be touched. The gangsters she had on her team were treacherous. They let their cannons bark, knocking the men down one by one like a bottle cans in a carnival game. The entire bar looked like a tragic massacre.

They went to the basement door and pulled it open only to be backed out by bullets flying their way. The basement was soundproof but the muffled sounds of gunshots had been heard and Eduardo already knew who was coming for him.

He had his own assault weapon and was spraying recklessly in their direction. Neither Indie or Ethic nor Chase could get through the door without getting chopped down.

"Yeah, motherfuckas! Fuck you, *putas!*" Eduardo screamed like a madman as he continued to shoot. He stood directly in front of YaYa, his back facing her as his focus was on the basement steps.

She knew that this was her only chance. If she didn't do something, Eduardo just might turn around and put a bullet in her head. He was feeling cornered and the slow torture he had planned was out the window. She still couldn't see him, letting her leave with her life. His thirst for revenge was too great. She contorted her body until she was used the gravity's momentum to swing herself back and forth. Her body went back and then as she pushed forward she kicked Eduardo with all her might. The force of her kick sent him flying forward, causing the old man to lose his balance as he went crashing to the floor. On cue, Ethic rounded the corner and put one bullet in Eduardo's head as he rushed past him, eyes focused only on YaYa. She finally cried when she saw his face and when he unhooked her, her naked body fell into his arms, helplessly.

The way she clung to him broke Indie's heart as he stood back watching in agony. It was clear. Ethic loved his woman and his woman loved Ethic in return. Indie's stupidity had caused him to lose the love of his life.

Chase stood back, flabbergasted as he looked back and forth between Ethic and Indie.

He thought that Indie would chop down Ethic where he stood, but instead he stepped aside and allowed Ethic to pass as he carried YaYa up the stairs.

"Yo, my man," Indie said.

Ethic looked back. "Take care of her," Indie finished.

Ethic nodded and then disappeared out of the bar. Indie had to reach out to grab hold of one of the chairs to stop himself from falling to his knees. It felt as if he had been sucker-punched in the gut. Sirens rang out in the distance.

"Let's go, big homie, it's over," Chase said. "I'm sorry."

"Me too," was Indie's only response.

Chapter 23

One Year Later

"I, Disaya Morgan, take this man to be my husband. To love and to cherish him. To find strength in his weakness, and to be the healing to his pain for the rest of the days of our lives," she said. This was the day she had dreamed of her entire life and as she stared at her husband, her soul mate, her other half, she realized that everything that she had been through had brought her to this moment. Through him, she was made whole again. After having her heart torn from her chest by betrayal, he had redeemed her. How amazing love was. She watched as her groom took the ring from his best man and placed it on her finger. It was his turn to recite his vows.

"I, Indie Perkins, take this magnificent woman as my wife. To love and protect. To provide for and to appreciate all the days of our lives. I will never forsake you for any other. No smile is as bright as the one that lights my life. You are my everything and I will be the man that you want me to be. I will be the husband you deserve and I will never love another the way that I love you. Thank you for this day, ma."

No others stood around them as they recited their vows. It was no big fanfare, the hood wasn't invited, no family, no friends, no children . . . just them, the pastor, and their love.

"With all the power vested in me, I now pronounce you man and wife. You may kiss your bride."

Indie poured his love into her as they kissed passionately. Tears ran down his face and he did nothing to wipe them away. He was so grateful for her love, for this second chance to love her right and he made a mental promise to himself to never get it wrong again.

As they walked out of the church hand in hand, nothing had ever felt so right. "I'm going to go to the ladies' room. I'll meet you at the car okay?"

He gave her hand a gentle squeeze and replied, "Hurry, ma. I don't want to be away from my wife for too long." He gave her a wink and she could see the pride in his eyes. He headed out of the church as she retreated inside the bathroom.

She went into one of the stalls and sighed in relief as her own tears formed in her eyes. Her entire life had been such a journey. She couldn't believe that she had even survived it all. Not Leah, not foster care, not the game, or the random men, or the fire, none of it had stopped her from attaining true happiness. Today, she was finally free of all pain. Her Prada Plan had finally come to fruition. She composed herself and then exited the stall only to halt in her step.

"You're beautiful," Ethic whispered.

She was speechless. She hadn't seen him since he had rescued her out of Eduardo's torture chamber yet here he was, as handsome as ever.

"You almost make me regret giving you to another man," Ethic said.

She wanted to fight the urge to touch him, but she couldn't; she rushed into his arms and he held her so tightly. She could tell that he missed her.

"I came to say good-bye, YaYa, and to take one last look at what I gave up," Ethic said.

"Why did you?" she asked, choking up. "Why did you send me back home to Indie? You made it seem like you and I had no future, but here you are. You love me. I can see it all over you. You wear your emotions like a coat, hanging from your shoulders. Why did you push me back into his arms?" she asked. "This could have been me and you."

Ethic caressed her chin and admired her beautiful face as he replied. "I love you, YaYa. More than I've ever loved anyone in a very long time, but you are his Raven. He feels for you the way I felt for her. I haven't fully healed from her death yet. I sent you home because it would have been selfish for me to make you stay but make no mistake about it, YaYa. I am in love with you."

He kissed her lips softly and as he pulled back he wiped away her tears. "Congratulations, baby girl, and good-bye."

She held on to his hand until space forced her to let go. Her heart ached with every step he took. He gave her that feeling and she wished that they had met before so that she would have had a chance to explore them, before he had met Raven or before she had met Indie, but the truth was, they both belonged to other people. "Next lifetime," she whispered.

He stopped walking and turned to her. He tossed her a black velvet box and she caught it out of midair. She opened it to find a brilliant diamond broach inside. She put her hand to her mouth. It was stunning. "Next lifetime," he replied. "My number will never change. If you ever need me, call."

He walked out and she let him. She pinned the broach to the bodice of her dress and then regained her composure before walking out of the bathroom. She found Indie, waiting near the car for his bride.

"You ready, Mrs. Perkins?" he asked.

"I'm ready, Mr. Perkins," she replied.

She dipped her head low and got into the car. As they pulled away from the church she fingered the broach with one hand while holding Indie's with the other. She loved Indie dearly. They had been through so much together and had beaten so many odds just to make it to this day. Still, despite all of this she pictured Ethic in her mind. Guilt filled her as she held onto Indie's hand. She was his new bride, his wife, and he was her everything, but the heart's wants were hard to ignore, and as Ethic's face clouded her mind, she couldn't help but wonder, *What if?*

"In the end life is not life without love from you."

—*Ashley Antoinette*

Ashley Antoinette Novels

The Prada Plan

The Prada Plan 2

The Prada Plan 3

Moth to a Flame

Guilty Gucci

ORDER FORM
URBAN BOOKS, LLC
97 N18th Street
Wyandanch, NY 11798

Name (please print):_____

Address: _____

City/State: _____

Zip: _____

QTY	TITLES	PRICE

Shipping and handling: add $3.50 for 1st book, then $1.75 for
each additional book.
Please send a check payable to:
Urban Books, LLC
Please allow 4-6 weeks for delivery